I0525666

Young, Black, Talented, & Alone

Chapter 2: The Trophy Chick

Relationships from a Male point of view

NATHAN ALEXANDER

Young, Black, Talented, and Alone

Copyright @ 2021 by Nathan Alexander

All rights reserved. No parts of this work may be reproduced or transmitted in any form or by any means, electronic or mechanical, including photocopying, or by any information storage or retrieval system, excerpt as it expressly is permitted by the Copyright Act or in writing from Nathan Alexander.

Disclaimer

The information published in this book represents the opinions, personal research, and business experience of the author. Since the success of anyone depends upon the skills and abilities of the person, the author makes no guarantees, and disclaims any personal loss or liabilities that may occur as a result of the use of the information contained herein.

This publication is designed to provide accurate and authoritative information in regard to the subject matter covered in it. It is provided with the understanding that the publisher is not engaged in rendering legal, accounting, or other professional services. If legal advice or other expert assistance is required, the services of a competent professional person should be sought.

ISBN-13: 978-0-578-83949-3

Table of Contents

And now…a word from Nate, ya'll…

Hello again everybody. This book is the second in my series, and deals with dating the "trophy chick." And what exactly is a "trophy chick", you may ask? The trophy chick is that woman that's real pretty on the outside, but crazy on the inside. They've been gassed up so much and for so long to believe they're all that, that behind closed doors, complexities, scheming and insecurities are constantly brewing in their pretty little heads of how to get over. I'm sure that it's because of how much larger than life guys have made them. They become objects instead of people. Then whenever they meet someone, those same insecurities and crazy traits manifest themselves into something destructive over and over again until it becomes a vicious cycle that's damn near impossible to break. I think it's because they haven't learned how to accept and love themselves FIRST. Gotta love yourselves first, ladies before you can love someone else.

That's how it was with Kaci, ol' girl in this book. Pretty on the outside, but on the inside, a straight nut. And I think it was because she hadn't learned how to balance life when we met. As a result, that crazy did manifest itself in destructive ways. While she was gorgeous, socially, emotionally, and environmentally, baby girl had a lot of stuff going on. And a lot of it was just bad. She was definitely an opportunist and a schemer. But even with scheming and using folk, she still had to pay for what she had done in the end. We all do. It's just a matter of when and where, and when it does happen, the majority of us probably don't think twice about all the things leading up to our payback. But if we just stop and think for a moment…it's really all relative.

As I said before, this book and this series book are my experiences with the types of women I dated in order to find what I really wanted in a mate. In my opinion, there are 4 types of women that every man seems to go through: the first love, the trophy chick, the work relationship, and the physical. This is Chapter 2, Book 2: The Trophy Chick. If you didn't buy the first one, go get it! Even though these are my stories, I feel that they can provide insight for both men and women on relationships and also let women know how men feel when we are in these types of relationships. Chapter 1 was a doozy, but this chapter is something else. And not only for the Black culture, but for everyone on the planet. For the men, it may be an "a-ha" moment, a moment to identify with that type of relationship. For the ladies, it may just be an epiphany, a chance to read and then think about a certain situation that you may have been in where you actually were the trophy chick to your man at the time. But then you messed things up…

Anyhoo, enjoy this chapter. And if you feel that you need to post an opinion, then by all means, please do so where this book is being sold. Amazon, that is. Stay tuned for Chapter 3, 'cuz it's definitely coming, so keep buying and keep reading!!! And for all of ya'll that bought my first book and have now bought this book, a big THANK YOU for keeping the faith by supporting and believing in me!

Nathan Alexander

I Knew a Girl Named
Kaci
Who was my
Trophy Chick…
Fine as a MF, but
Crazy as HELL,
A young girl
Who thought her game
was
SLICK!
(or that's what she
believed…)

I.

So...One Night in the Parking Lot...

Aw yeah, Nineteen Ninety One, the year when things just *couldn't* have gotten any better! Here I was, twenty one, livin' in the A-T-L, had just graduated from college, and for the most part had escaped most of the traps that so many Black men before me had gone through: I never went to jail, never got in trouble with the law, never been shot or wounded in some bullshit dispute, and never been in the wrong place at the wrong time to get involved in some other bullshit .

Didn't have no babies, no babies' mommas to pay child support to, and wasn't on drugs or an alcoholic. Wasn't gay or on the down-low, and didn't have no HIV virus; finished high school AND college, and finally was on a good job until I could find a better one. At that time, my mind was in party mode all the freakin' time, and party I did. Oh yeah. LIFE WAS GOOD.

So me and my boys used to party at this college club in Decatur (Dee-kay-tur/also known as Tha Deck), called Club XS, and everybody who was anybody used to be there. And even if you weren't "somebody," you could still be the man or the woman while in there. It was just that kind of vibe. Folks from school, girls from the fashion college, and the locals who were just cool and looked forward to having a good time were all up in there. It was at the time, mucho ghetto fabuloso, but you could find a little bit of anything and everything up in there. And, you could also find me there each and every (and I do mean EVERY) Friday and Saturday night. It was only five dollars to get in, even after midnight, so I could afford this little luxury of mine.

And for you brothas readin' this, some of the FINEST women in the A used to come and get their party on with us. They were fine, but they were down for whatever. Women who were cool and didn't care what you did for a living, didn't give a damn what kind of car you drove. They were just down-to-earth, easy to talk to, and anxious to have a good time. This was the time in the A when you could just walk up to a chick and just start dancing with her, no hesitation. You could also ask for her number, and odds were 70 to 30 you'd walk away from her with it in your hand. What a time to be young and alive! Or so I thought...

At the time, I had just broken up with my ex, Cute Face over at Spelman, and I was searchin' for somethin' different. You know, when you always look for somethin', sometimes it can only bring you trouble, as opposed to not looking for it and having the Man Upstairs bring it right to you. Looking back, you always appreciate the latter, 'cuz the way that person is brought to you will most always bring you peace of mind rather than the former, which will just make your head hurt and drive you crazy as well. However, when I met Kaci, she definitely fell into the former zone.

So one fateful night, me and my boy Matt were outside in the parking lot at XS, sittin' in the car, drinkin' and chillin'. Matt didn't drink but I sure as hell did. This was back when I used to be able to *drank*, and drank I did. I used to be into those "forties" real hard, and was on my second one that night when I saw her. Matter of fact, I first saw her outta my rearview mirror, walkin' towards the club, and baby girl was lookin' GOOD.

I was good and lit, so I did what any brotha in a parking lot who had a buzz who saw a fine-ass girl would do: I got out of the car and yelled like a damn fool for her to come over. Looking back, I thought she wasn't gonna step to me, but she did, sho'nuff Shawty. And since she started coming over, I had to represent. I got back in the car, while she strolled on over and looked in.

"Whassup?" she asked. Damn, she looked even better close up.

"Wassup, Shawty?" I said, blinkin' at her through bloodshot eyes. "Lookin' all good and shit."

"Ain't nothin' Tryin' to look good enough to get up in this club," she said, grinning like a Cheshire cat. She turned around so I could see her outfit. Girl had on a catsuit. Meow-Wow.

"I look good, folk?" she asked. Boy, did she?

"Sho'nuff, Shawty," I said, lookin her up and down at butt level. So What'cho name is, girl?"

"Kaci," she said sweetly. She didn't step away either. That was my first clue that she might've been interested.

"True dat," I said. "I knew a girl named Kaci…" I sang. She rolled her eyes and sighed.

"Don't, okay?" she said. "You wouldn't believe how many times people have sang that song to me. I'ma go to Minneapolis and strangle Prince."

"Right, right. It just sounds like 'Nikki'." She looked at me strangely. Then,

"Naw. It don't." Like I was saying, I was lit up like a Christmas tree, but she was fine.

"Okay, well maybe it don't. So ummm… you goin' up in there tonight, right?"

"Hell yeah," she said, grinning again. Damn, as fine as she was, I couldn't just let her walk away without trying.

"Well, umm…"I stammered, "Before you go in, can I… like… get yo' number? I mean, you know, if that's cool with you?" She flashed that smile again.

"Yeah, that's cool. You got a pen?"

"Whaat? Do I?" I said, openin' the dash and feelin' around for one. "Better believe it." But after watching me search for the longest, Matt rolled his eyes, and pulled one out of his pocket. "Here, man," and that was all he said. I just looked at him. Hell, he could've handed me one in the first place instead of makin' me look stupid. He was such a hater. I glanced back over to her and smiled.

"Here you go, Sexy," I said, handing her the pen, taking her all in. She took it and wrote her number on some type of post-it or something. Meanwhile, her friend that she was walking with was growing impatient, just huffin'. I did not give a DAMN at that point.

"Come on, girl," her friend hinted. "Let's go."

"Girl, I'm comin'." She peeled it off and handed it back to me. Shit…wasn't my fault her friend couldn't pull nobody. Her friend looked down in the car at Matt and smiled. Matt looked away. Seemed like ol' girl just couldn't win. Both of them started walking away. Kaci looked back and gave me a tiny wave.

"See you in the club." She didn't ask my name but gave me the digits.

OKAY. WHO WAS <u>THE</u> MAN? ME!!!

That's when Matt noticed that Kaci still had her pen.

"Ay!" Matt yelled out. "That's my pen! Run it back!" All three of us looked at him like he was crazy. They giggled, but they came back to bring his funky little pen. I was lit, but still embarrassed. They passed it to me and I threw it to him.

"Matt, man, calm down. Here's your little pen back. Stop actin' like a little girl, okay? You see I'm tryin' to do business here. Sellin' some opportunity."

Kaci giggled. Matt sulked.

"Makin' thangs happen," I continued. "Anyway, ignore him. He's just sensitive." And again a smile.

"'Kay." That was a good sign I guess, smiling but not leaving. I looked down at the paper, and my eyes got wide.

"Girl, this ain't yo real number!" The smile changed to a "Huh?"kind of look.

"Yes it is. Why you say that?"

"'Cuz…I ain't never seen no number that starts with a four."

"I don't know 'bout that. But it's my number."

"Hmmm. So…okay. If I call it, you gon' answer?"

"Either me or my mom or my brother. Somebody gon' answer it!"

"And this ain't no Dial-a-Joke?'"

She shrugged. "Call and see. That's all I'ma say."

"I will." I motioned to Matt. "Matt, will you do the honors?"

"Yeah, yeah."

What was up with the attitude? Disregarding that, he whipped out his cell phone and gave it to me. I began to dial. It was the right number, 'cuz it said her name, her momma's, and her brother's name all on the greeting. She looked at me with the old 'told you so' face.

"See? Told you it was the right number. So what's up? Ya'll comin' inside or what?"

"We gon' come through in a little bit. You gon' save me a dance?"

"I can do that. Just come on in."

"I got you, girl. We'll be there in a few."

"Okay, then."

And then she walked on with her girl, and I got a good look at the back. Damn, it was boomin'! She definitely had ass, and not too many redbones have that. You know, the ghetto booty. Most Reds usually have chest, but no ass. Dr. FreakNasty had chest galore, but when she turned around? An ironing board. But the good Lord ALWAYS makes exceptions, and I saw one there. She must've been a mutant.

"Damn, Matt. Look at that."

"Look at what?" He was looking around, waiting for us to go in.

"She got ass." He looked over his shoulder and caught a glimpse.

"Oh yeah," he said, checking her out. "And her friend too. But her girl looked like a dude. I don't think that…"

"Man, we definitely got to go up in there tonight," I said, cutting him off. I opened my bottle again. "Lemme finish tappin' this, and I'll be straight."

"I'm already straight," he said. I turned it up and finished that little corner of beer that was left.

"Yeah, me too. Let's roll." We got out of the ride. I stumbled and lumbered all the way up to the door, but we made it.

II.

All Up IN the Club…

We went up to the door, got frisked, paid and headed on in. Music was pumpin' and everybody and their momma was on the floor. We walked around, looking for Kaci and friend.

"Man, I don't see her ass at all. Hell she go to?" I screamed to Matt over the music.

"Don't know?" he yelled back. "But I'm fixin' to grab me somebody's daughter up in here!"

"You can't!" I said. "You gotta help me find ol' girl!"

"Damn, she in here! Just keep walkin' around!" And then, true to his word, he grabbed somebody's daughter that walked by and pulled her on the floor. Some friend, I'll tell ya. As for me, I kept walkin' around this camp, searchin'. When the next song came on, nobody left the dance floor. Instead, more people got on and the floor quickly got packed to the limit. The dance floor also had these big wooden painted boxes you could dance on top of. And on top of one of the boxes was Kaci, dancin' her ass off with some brotha, and Matt on another box, shakin' his ass with the girl he pulled.

"Kaci!" She couldn't hear me. A little louder then.

"Kaci!" Still couldn't hear me. I took a huge breath and then shouted it out.

"KA-CAY!" I screamed to her. She looked down and around, giving me that deer stuck in the headlights look. That was good, because at least she heard me in the middle of the music that was seriously pounding. I waved my hand. "Over here! Ka-Cay! Ay! Tryin' to holla at ya, girl!"

She finally looked my way and waved. Then she hopped down off the box, left ol'boy standin' there, and ran right over to me. There was that smile again.

"Hey!"

"Hey." I thought you weren't coming in for awhile. I got scared."

"Me too. 'Specially when I saw you up there with other dude. I thought you weren't gonna come down."

"Well here I am."

"Dat's wassup, then."

"I hear ya."

By now another party-rocker jam had come on. Folks stampedin' to the floor again, runnin' into us, tryin' to pack the floor before it went off. Still we were trying to talk over the music to each other. But it's kinda hard tryin' to do that and you gotta keep screamin'. Do that and let the music cut off. You sound crazy as hell. But back to the conversation.

"What's your name?" she said. "I don't even know it! I just gave a stranger my number!"

"It's Al!"

"Hal?"

"No! AL!" We're still screamin'.

"Like in 'Married with Children' Al? Like Al Bundeee?"

"Somethin' like that! So now we ain't strangers!" I kept screaming. And then the music cut off, and people were starin' at me while I said that in mid-sentence. I must've looked like a crazy man. How embarrassing.

"Got it." Pause. Then another song came on. Kaci's head started bobbin', people started dancing, they took their eyes offa me, and that ass of hers started shakin' again.

"You like that song right there, huh?" I yelled.

"Ooh boy, yuh. That's it right there!" she yelled back.

"Is? You wanna dance?" I asked. Man, this chick was workin' it!

I didn't have to ask twice. She took my hand and drug me to the floor. Guess she wanted to shake it. And shake it she did.

Now I know for a fact that I'm a good dancer. I know that 'cuz I improvise a lot. Don't let Soma's comments fool you from the first chapter. The way it's supposed to be here in the South is that the man just stands there and does his little dance, while the woman is the star, shakin' it all around him. In other words, she becomes the show while the man is like the pole or the prop.   Not with me and Kaci, though. We got on the floor and burned it up. By the time we decided to leave, we had a circle around us, checkin' our moves. I'll give it to her…Kaci could go. I guess that in addition to her looks and booty, that that dancing was an additional turn-on for me. When we finally left the floor, dudes were tryin' to holler at her, and women were pinching my ass. After awhile, the circle finally disappeared and everybody was back to shakin' their asses with their partners, sans Al and Kaci. I felt that we really looked good together out there tonight, and from there, we just felt a vibe. At least I know I did.

So we headed to the bar to get a couple of drinks, made some more small talk, got better acquainted, got our stuff and went back to the edge of the dance floor to people-watch. I looked around and saw Matt back out there, still shakin' his ass like his life depended on it, sweatin' like hell with some new chick he just snatched up. I just shook my head in disbelief.

When the slow drag number came on, it was back to the floor. By this time, I was lit up like a candle, with so much alcohol in me so I was feelin' the urge, and that's when Winky woke up. Wide awake and ready for action as we pressed our bodies into a serious grind. I know that it states in laws of physics that no two objects can occupy the same space at the same time, but we damn sure tried.

We were literally makin' love on that floor, with clothes on. Kaci felt Winky pressing up against her, but she didn't look surprised or try to \ leave. Instead she got closer and whispered in my ear.

"It's so hard," she said, and then started rubbing all on it. I wanted to say 'I'm out!' so bad, take her to a hotel, but I played it cool.

"Ain't it though?" I said. "I don't think you can handle it."

"And that's why you should call me." When she said that, Winky went from mild to rock damn hard. He could've smashed through a brick wall. I looked at her. "Oh yeah, I'ma definitely do that."

"You'd better." And when that song was over, the club was over. We headed out the door and back into the last hours of the night.

"Don't forget," she said, walking away . "I'ma need you to call me."

"Sheeeet, you think I won't? Hell yeah, I'ma call!" Then, "Hold up. I don't see your girl, so…can…can I walk you to your car?" I asked. The grin broke out again and she wrapped her arm around mine.

"Come on." Yea-yuh, a brotha was in!

As we strolled along, I was askin' all kinda questions, mostly tryin' to see where her head was at. "So whassup? You got a man or what?" I asked.

"Had one, but you know how that goes."

"Well, yeah, but naw, not in your case. Fine lil' thang like yourself must have plenty of brothas chasin' you."

"I did, but we moved. And yeah, a lot of guys chase me, but I don't give 'em no play. For what? Hard to trust dudes in Atlanta."

"So you not from here, then?"

"Nope. All the way from Augusta, Georgia."

"Ohhhh. Well, all right then." Augusta, huh? We continued walking and finally reached her car. It was a Ford Escort GT. That was the most popular teen/young adult car at the time in the A. Everybody had one. Everybody except me. I had a Celica.

"Nice ride," I said.

"Thanks. But it ain't mine." She walked around to the passenger side. I opened up the door for her (see, chivalry wasn't dead!) and she got her cute lil' sexy ass in there, along with the rest of her. She looked over to the driver's side and saw her friend walking up. I looked down at her, my hands playing out a little drumbeat on top of the roof. We were both smiling.

"You gon' call me, right?" she asked again. Was that a trick question?

"And you know this!"

Her girl didn't say nothin', just got in and slammed the door.

"And when we gon' go out?"

"Shiiit, how 'bout next week?" Her girl, who was being ignored, cleared her throat and started up the car. She glared at me, and I stepped back.

"Damn, Kaci…what's up with your girl?"

"Nothin'. She just mad 'cuz she didn't get no play tonight."

"Hello! No Play still here! Good night, then!" her girl yelled out while slammin' the car into reverse, puttin' it in drive, and proceeding to burn rubber out of the parking lot. Clearly baby girl had issues. She really looked like a dude in heels. Was it my fault she looked manly? It's been my experience that when girls act like that, it's because of two things I know of: One: Your friend that comes once a month is stopping by, or Two: NOBODY wants to be bothered with you in the club. Because you look like a damn dude! I figured that Reason Number Two was correct, 'cuz Kaci's girl was kinda unattractive. Better yet, she looked like a dude in stilettos. There, I said it.

But that's how it goes with women: Ugly will always hang with cuties. Don't trip though: guys do it too. But it's always a pack of hoo-ha's who have that one shining star, and that star usually hangs out because they have insecurities about themselves. But I didn't care and really couldn't worry about that one. I had the passenger's number, and the passenger was FIIINE and cute to boot.

I didn't give a description of Kaci, except for the booty, 'cuz that's what blinded me. But here it is: She was light-skinned, with almost Hispanic features. When you looked at her, she put you in the mind of Rosie Perez, no lie. She could've literally been her twin, stunt double, or something. She was cute, had a beautiful smile, and seemed to be interested in a brotha, so I didn't hesitate to come up for a come up. For all of ya'll that don't know what this means, it meant one thing for me: OPPORTUNITY!!

The only thing I couldn't figure out was why. I mean, Kaci was a beautiful girl, and I'm not an ugly dude. But I don't have movie star looks. I'm just an ordinary Joe. But it was interesting that she chose me. So maybe she saw in me something out of the ordinary.

Didn't matter. We were getting ready to hook things up.

III.

The Pilgrimage

The very next day, I called her and we just vibed. But as we talked, I found out that she suffered from what I like to call the "mirror syndrome." And exactly what is that, you may ask? Practically everybody falls victim to it when they meet somebody for the first time. And it all stems from trying to give that good first impression. Some examples from our conversation that night:

"So …what you like to do, Al?"

"I like to go to comedy movies."

"Really? Me too! What else?"

"Oh, I don't know. Go and watch the Braves play?"

"Really? I love watchin' 'em play! Anything else?"

That's when I decided to screw with her head. "Yeah. I like fantasizing about two James Brown impersonators and Grace Jones getting together and doing the Watutsi on my back with bell bottoms, stack shoes and spiked heels, singing 'Get Up Offa That Thang'."

But it was no use.

"You're kidding!" she said. "That's one of my fantasies, too! We have so much in common!"

Yeah right. Youse a lie. Ya'll know good and damn well that dudes in their twenties only pretend to be interested in what females like, knowing that we don't really give a fat rat's ass about any of it. We only pretend so we can try to tap that ass as the ultimate goal. And in reality, women do it too, but that's because they think they see potential. Smart men, similar interests, good dick… it's all relevant.

But the trip part is when women also think, "Well damn, he's got some weird habits…but I can change him. I can fix that."

It's so interesting how women see us as their own personal project to "fix." And it always happens in the beginning when things are new and going ever so well. Same situation throughout time, only now it's me and Kaci playing the parts.

Man, she pretended to be SO interested in what I was doing and saying that night, and I did the same. Just lyin' on both ends to stay on each other's good side. That's a damn shame. I was so lit that I just came right out and told her she was fine, and she told me I was sexy. Really? When she said that shit, my ego elevated to Cloud Nine. I offered up a date to her, and she accepted. So yes, we were goin' out! I just couldn't believe it, 'cuz she was so diabolically pretty. A trophy girl, if you would, who I thought would've never chose me in life's lineup. I thought she was out of my league, simply by the way she looked. I also thought that she was one of those high-maintenance women. But all that was out the door, 'cuz she said yes to me! But back to the convo.

"Soooo….where you wanna go?"

"Don't matter," she said. "I just wanna hang out with you. You know, spend a little time."

WHAAAT?? "A'ight then," I said. "Next Saturday. I'll pick you up 'round nine."

"I can't wait 'til then. Come see me at work on Friday. I get off at midnight."

"I can do that. Where you work at?"

"I ain't gon' tell ya."

"Why?" I asked. "You ashamed?"

"Kinda. I'm just gonna give you directions, and when you get there, you be the judge."

That shit kinda made me think. Work. Night. Off at midnight. Hmmm...

"You ain't no stripper, right?"

"Would it matter if I was?"

"Naw. Naw, it wouldn't. Wouldn't matter one way or another." Ya'll, I was lyin' like a rug. Hell yeah it would've mattered! Ain't no tellin' what kinda tricks she may have learned and turned! All in the club! You know that dollar is a mu'fucka, as well as the root of all evil. Couldn't bring her to my momma's house either. A stripper? Hell to the naw. But still...she was fine.

"Good," she said slowly, and paused. Then all of a sudden, there came this laugh, complete with all this snorting and crackin' up.

"I had you goin', didn't I?" she asked.

I pretended to laugh my ass off, then stopped. "Naw, 'cuz I knew you wasn't no stripper. You look too classy to be a stripper."

"Really?" I could tell she was brightening up on the other end of the phone. "Well, if I look so classy, you're gonna be in for a big surprise when you come to the job."

"But you ain't no stripper, right?"

She sighed. "Just come to the job, about twelve. Okay, honey?"

"I'll be there."

She gave me directions, we said our goodbyes and got off the phone.

YES!!! I HAD A DATE WITH KACI!!! LIFE IS SWEET!!

Now here's where the long distance comes in. Maaan, I just didn't know how far I had to travel just to see her. Lemme tell ya, it was a lonnnng way from where I lived! Norcross, Georgia for Chrissakes! And I lived in the city! But first, lemme explain something. First and foremost, I'm from Atlanta, born and raised, but (and I know this is gonna cause the people reading this to say '*Damn, Atlantans are stupid*,' but hey, deal with it) there are just some spots in the city where you just don't go. And it was hard for me to travel out there, due to my comfort zone. But you limit yourself in that regard. You may meet a chick you can possibly vibe with, but once you find out where she lives, it may just be too far to really vibe with. You'll see in a minute. Between writing those directions down and actually getting out there, I discovered it was really way too far for my tastes…

But she was fine. Fine goes a long way.

So anyway, my area of comfort was downtown Atlanta. Her job was *wayyyy* the fuck out in the boonies. I'm talking like Jimmy Carter Boulevard, Norcross, Georgia, fill-up-first-before-you-go-out-there area. One way was like forty-six miles, and traveling there? You might as well pack a suitcase. But it's interesting what we as guys will do just to try something new. When people who live in the city just hear the name 'Norcross', they know for a fact it's way the fuck out. But you REALLY know it's far when the MARTA train don't go out there, 'cuz back then, they hadn't even laid track for it. That's how far away it was.

When we started dating, it was late 1991, and not only was it was way out there to travel, but living there? You could tell that we definitely weren't welcome as a mass exodus. A few Black folk were okay, like a dash of pepper on egg whites, but a lot? That's what they feared MARTA would bring and they wasn't havin' it.

Think about it: Black folks havin' a way into white folks' country without spending for gas? That would fuck up some serious shit. They already had an abbreviation for MARTA: 'Moving Africans Rapidly Through Atlanta' and beyond. To sum it up, they just didn't want that 'beyond' phrase connecting to them. And like I was sayin', Black folk who lived in the city already knew how far away Norcross was!

So once I found out where Kaci lived and decided to make a pilgrimage, I said to myself: *Self, if she seem like she ain't worth it, don't start shit. It's ninety-two miles round trip, and sooner or later, all that travelin's gonna wear your ride out!*

Self was like, "Okay."

I was sayin' this to myself all the way to her job. And when I finally came up to where she worked, I was shocked.

No, baby girl wasn't a stripper. But she did work the fries and cash register at a very well-known fast-food joint. I was trippin'. Fine and cute as this girl was, and she was smellin' like Parfum de la Potatoe? I felt like I was in the Twilight Zone. It couldn't be real, but it was, ya'll. When I came in the door, she was takin' a customer's order.

Then she saw me, and the Cheshire Cat grin spread over her face again.

"Hey, Honey!" she yelled, skinnin' and grinnin' at me.

"Wassup girl." I was excited to see her, but I played it cool.

"Hold up a minute." She turned back to her customer. "That'll be five seventy nine. You want fries with that?" she asked. The customer nodded, gave the money, she gave him change and then walked to the back. I could hear her callin' out, "Fries up!" and saw her dump the fries into the fry bin. Oh Hell naw!

She walked back to the cash register and waited until the burgers were done. She had already put his fries on the tray, and I peeped them. They were layin' all greasy. The burgers came up, and once she got his, she slid the tray over.

"Have a nice night," she said.

By this time, I walked back to a booth, waiting on her. She saw me, came on over and stood by the table. I started talkin'.

"So this your spot, huh?"

"Yeah. You can't get rich off of it, but at least it's steady."

Ohhhh-kayyy. "Yeah, you right about that," I said, sniffing her. "Damn girl, you smell good! Almost like one of those value meals up there." I pulled her to me.

"Quit it! You so silly!"

"Right, right. So what time you get off?"

"About thirty more minutes. Why? You wanna take me home?"

"Hell yeah, I'd love to. I love having the smell of food in my ride, 'cuz it makes me hungry as hell!"

"It does?" she said. She kissed me and then, "Hungry for me? Where are my manners? You want something to eat?"

"Ummmm…yeah, if you wanna hook it up. I wasn't tryin' to impose or nothing…"

"Relax," she said, kissing me again. This time on the cheek and then licking me in my ear. "It's on me."

"A'ight then," I said softly. She already had me when she kissed me.

She got out of my grip and walked back over to the counter. Damn, even in her fast-food outfit, she looked good. That booty was boomin' in those damn navy blue, hemmed-at-the-bottom, polyester work dickies.

She came back with the food, sat it down in front of me and went back to clean up before she left. Ah, another view of that ass. *So refreshing*, I thought as I ate. What more could a brotha want? Free food, money, a car, and a girl who looked good, with an ass outta this world, who smelled like food. I could only imagine how she looked with her clothes off.

Wouldn't be long before wondering turned into reality, please believe.

She was finally ready to go, so we headed out the door, into the ride. I opened up her side first and let her get in. I had to give it to her; even the way she slinked in was sexy. As we were riding, we made small talk about a little bit of everything.

I still couldn't get over how we met. She told me that she hoped I thought she wasn't slutty, dancing all up on me and grabbing Winky when she didn't even know me. I didn't. I just told her that I thought she was bold and adventurous. I also asked her if she danced like that with anyone else that night? She told me it had happened only one other time, but outside of that, the answer was no.

Bullshit. I think guys of all races have always heard that lie in some form or fashion, haven't we? I know that *I've* heard it as much as I've told it. Then she told me that I was special. I asked her what made her want to give *me* her number; an ordinary, drunk-ass brother out in the parking lot who was yellin' to her to come over?

"I don't know," she said. "I just thought you were cute. And I liked our conversations we had on the phone afterwards."

"So if that's the case, can we really do this?" I asked. "Can we really get to know each other, hook up and be boyfriend and girlfriend?"

"I don't see why not," she responded. "You seem like you got a good head on your shoulders, and you don't look like a player, so I don't think there'd be problems."

"Nah," I said. "When's your next day off?"

"Sunday."

"Okay. So let's make somethin' happen on Sunday."

"Like what?"

"I don't know. Since this'll be like our second date…"

"Second? When was the first?"

"Me takin' you home right now."

"Oh." There was that grin again.

"Like I was sayin'," I continued. "Maybe we could do something Sunday, like goin' to get somethin' to eat and then catchin' a movie."

"And then what?"

"What you mean?" I asked.

"The movie. What's gonna happen after the movie?"

Damn, was she hinting at something? I really hadn't thought that far ahead. Trying to be a gentleman here.

"Well, umm…" I was waffling. "I figure that we could go back over to your house, strip, and then have hot, butt-naked, unprotected sex." Kidding of course, but her eyes got big. "I'm kidding," I said. "I hope I didn't offend you."

"You didn't, but don't kid like that."

"I'm sor--"

"Cuz you got me hot." She stared at me with a come-hither look. "Don't start nothin' you can't finish," she continued, and put her hand on Winky again. He jumped up, all excited, as if to say '*Whassup, Shawty? Who's that touching me?*" The statement she made and that gesture turned me on full throttle, but I didn't show it. Only Winky, who was now a rock in my drawers, knew how I felt.

"Bay-bay" I said, "EVERY thing I start, I finish. Believe that."

"I hear you, Daddy. Turn right here." I turned into the apartments where she stayed. "Park right here." I parked in the area where there was very little lighting. She started to open the door, so I jumped out and ran my happy ass over to her side.

"Lemme get that for you." I opened her door, took her by the hand and led her out of the car. She got out, still smellin' like fries but still lookin' good, even in the night. "Can I walk you up the stairs?" I asked.

"Sure." We walked up and stood by the door. All of a sudden, she reached out and gave me a hug.

"Thanks for taking me home. Usually my mom picks me up or I bum a ride with one of my co-workers."

"Yeah, that's a good thing, to know that you have co-workers who'll do that for you. And it don't hurt either that you don't live but ten minutes away from your job."

"True." She reached into her purse for her key.

"So Sunday, then?" she asked.

"Yep. Sunday it'll be."

"I'll be waiting."

"And I'll be here." Pause on both our ends.

"All right, then," I said.

"Okay." We were again at an awkward moment. I didn't know if she wanted to kiss me or if I were to try and kiss her without gettin' my face slapped or karate-kicked. But there we were, and I took a chance. I leaned in, not expecting her to return the favor, but she did, and the kiss was good. She didn't smack me across the face or nothin'. Instead, she just smiled, still lookin' like Rosie Perez.

"Goodnight," I said, walking backwards down the steps.

"Night-night," she said, walking in the door.

You know I waited to see all of that back until the door closed. I was ready to bring it to the floor with this chick. Not next Sunday, but right now. I couldn't wait.

IV.

We Ready!

Next Sunday came, and I was ready. When I got home during the wee morning hours after a night of partying with the fellas at XS again, I called Kaci and we talked about what kind of movies we liked and what kinda records we listened to. In doing so, we both discovered that our favorite musical artist of all time was Prince.

"Damn, you're a Prince fan?!" she asked in disbelief.

"Sho'nuff. Been one since 'Dirty Mind'."

"Oh yeah, I love Prince. He's a musical genius."

"No doubt. I think that once he's gone, historians will probably end up callin' him like the Twentieth Century Mozart, 'cuz that's what he is."

"You right. He's sexy as hell, too."

"Well, Kace, I don't know about that part. I do know, however that the brother is talented. Gifted even."

"Oh yeah. Definitely. So…what time you comin' to get me?"

"Probably around eight. You gonna be ready?"

"Oh yeah. I'll be ready."

"Cool. I'ma jump offa this line, and I'll see you at eight."

"'Kay. Bye."

Brotha Man took a shower, laid out his clothes and lotioned, brushed, and cologned it up. I was ready. I even vacuumed my car out so it didn't smell like fresh fries no more. Now I was really ready. I took off towards Norcross again, and along the way, I took care to moisten up the lips, chew some gum for the fresh breath, and take some tissue to mine the rest of those remaining boogers out. For those of you who don't know, people who live in Georgia suffer incredibly from sinus problems, and we are *constantly* blowing our noses in order to breathe. As I was blowing, a couple of boogies got caught on my shirt. So after that, I got 'em offa there, checked myself fully and threw the tissue out the window so that all would be cool.

When I got to her apartments and walked up to the door, I heard a crash and some women hollering. I lightly tapped on the door.

"Who the fuck is it?!" a voice hollered out.

"It's Al," I said, quietly. Kaci came bustin' out the door, stompin' hard in those little sandals she had on. She looked like she was pissed.

"Hi," I said.

"Yeah, a'ight. I'm ready. Let's go. Fuck this shit!"

She stormed down the walkway and to the car. *All right then,* I thought. She acted like she was pissed so I just went down and opened the door for her, went 'round to my side and got in. We rolled out. As we were driving, she didn't say one word. The silence was making me uncomfortable, so I finally spoke up.

"What's wrong with you, girl?" She didn't say nothin', so I tried again. "Hey. I said…what's wrong with you?"

She just kept staring straight ahead and sighing. Then finally, a word. "Nothin'. Nothin' except the fact that my brother is a stupid-ass mu'fucka."

"Damn. What happened?"

From that point, it all flowed out. "He gon' try and stand up to my momma, callin' her a bitch and sayin' that she ain't shit," she pushed out.

"Mmmm."

"And then," she continued, "He thought he was gonna try and fight her."

"Whaat? How old's your brother?"

"Nigga's thirteen!"

"Thirteen? He must be a bad mu'fucka. So when he tried to do that, what'd YOU do?"

She glared at me. "What'd I do? I kicked his ass! Took a coffee mug and busted it upside his head! Cold cocked his ass! Shit, I wish he would've tried to hurt my momma! I swear, Al, I swear to God that if he had hurt her, I would've killed his ass!"

"Only thirteen, though."

"You havta understand my brother. He's got a real bad temper when he gets mad. And when he gets mad, nigga gets wild, or tries to."

"Sounds to me like he needs a man to kick his ass. Want me to do it?"

"Nah, 'cuz then Momma be done called the police on you, and she ain't even met you yet. Her or my brother."

"I feel you girl. Damn, I'm sorry that your brother had to go and fuck up your evening. It's too bad, 'cuz you really look nice tonight."

She did, too. Know how I mentioned that we were both Prince fans? Tonight she dressed like one of his many women. She had the white ruffled shirt on, complete with some black cat pants and some patent leather black heels. It was hard for me to have a conversation with her about her brother when she was looking so damn good, but I tried.

"I know that what he did was bad," I continued, "But don't let that take your focus off of us having a good time tonight."

And just like that, the grin came back. "Don't worry," she quipped. "My mind is already a million miles away from that bullshit."

"Good, good," I said.

"So…what are we doin' tonight?"

"Well, I thought that maybe we'd catch a movie and then get somethin' to eat."

"Sounds good."

"Oh yeah. It is." We continued driving. When we were almost there, I gave her a rule. "Now close your eyes, 'cuz we're almost there." I guess in her mind she thought we were goin' to the IMAX theater or that place where they serve you dinner while you watch the movie, 'cuz she sure dressed the part. When we got there, I was like, "Now open them." She opened them up and her eyes got big.

"What's wrong?" I asked.

"Nothin'."

"You said you wanted to see a movie, right?"

"Yeah, but…"

"But what?"

"Nothin'. I just thought that we would've gone to that movie place and had dinner while we watched the movie, instead of comin' here to the dollar fifty. I could've gone with my brother here."

"That right? So what'cha sayin'?"

"I think that I'm a little overdressed for here, don'tcha think?"

"Nahhh, you look good. Matter of fact, you'd look good if you went to the theater like Eve, butt naked and all."

She laughed. That was good. "Thanks. I needed that. But still, I feel overdressed."

I rolled my eyes. "Aw, come on girl! Ain't nobody gonna be worried 'bout what you got on. Let's just go and watch the movie." I got out the car, went around to her side and opened the door. Then I took her by the hand and lifted her out oh-so-gently.

"Come on."

"'Kay." We went on in. I must admit, she DID stand out. Not because she was lookin' good, but because of what she had on. From the time we were at the ticket booth to the time we were at the snack bar, all you heard from brothas as well as my Hispanic brethren was, "Damn!" "Got-damn!" "Aiee! Muy caliente! She's hot, Ese!" "Damn, she fine!"

She pretended not to like it, but you know, pretty girls' egos soak that shit up like a sponge. Cheshire cat all the way when dudes were talkin'.

"C'mon, let's go," I said. I know she didn't want to, but she went anyway.

"'Kay." We went on into the movies. The movie was good, but when we came out, it was the same thing all over again. The catcalls continued until we got back in the car. Even then, brothas were watching us drive off and just a-wavin'. I had a real hot tamale on my hands!

"That was fun," she said. "But I'm hungry. Where we goin' to eat?"

"Oh, don't worry 'bout that," I said. "I got the spot."

"But where are we…" She looked out and saw where we were. "Oh no!"

"What? I said that I was gonna take you to get somethin' to eat, and here we are!"

"Yeah, but I thought we were goin' to a sit-down restaurant!"

"What? You got somethin' against drive-thrus?"

"No, but…"

"But what then?"

The drive-thru person came on the loudspeaker. "May I take your order, please?"

"Nothin'. Forget it." She was upset, but she'd be all right.

"May I take your order, please?" came the voice from the loudspeaker

"Okay. What you want, then?" Kaci didn't like the restaurant, but guess what? She was hungry, and she wasn't no fool. She ordered a bunch of food, and then tore that shit up. Hell, I had to keep my hands and fingers away, else she probably would've bit my ass.

When I finally got her home, it was around twelve-thirty. She was like, "Thank you, honey. It's been interesting."

"You welcome, baby." Man, I took her to a movie *and* got her something to eat? Time to make that play, Shawty. She got out and I walked her to the door. We both stood there for a minute.

"Can I come in?" I said.

"No. I'm really tired. Plus my mom and brother might wake up."

"Don't worry. I'll be very quiet. I'm a silent lover, girl."

"Oh naw, Shawty, that's all right. But guess what?"

"What's that, baby girl?" I asked.

"You can watch me up in the window of my room."

"Watch you do what?"

"You'll see. Flash your lights to let me know it's you."

"A surprise, huh? Are you serious?"

"Sure am. You can drive around to the back. That's where my room is."

"Cool."

She went on in, and I took my happy ass back to the car and got in. *Aw shit, now...a real-live peep show!* I thought. I burned rubber all in the apartment complex tryin' to get back there so fast. Two minutes after we had spoken, there she was in the window.

I think at that time in my life there was nothing else in the world sweeter than a girl who was down to do whatever with you. And she wanted to show off the goods. I saw her lookin' out, so I flashed my lights. She waved, and I could also see her grin at me. I think she put some music on, 'cuz she started swaying and taking off each piece of clothing, starting with her pants. She had on these lace white panties and turned her ass round to the window.

Damn.

Then she turned back around and off came the shirt. Double damn! Kaci was fine. And then...

Then she slid a black teddy on over her panties and bra.

Huh?

I thought I was gonna see me some skin. Guess not, 'cuz after the teddy was on, *then* the panties and bra came off. Hmmm. Winky was a rock by now, but I guess she just wanted me to fantasize for the moment so she could have me guessin' about what I may be gettin' eventually.

I had to use my imagination, 'cuz she didn't reveal a damn thang in that teddy. No nipple, no nothin'. And then…then she had the nerve to wave goodnight and turn out the damn lights. What a rip-off! But you know, a brotha did get to see the draws, so that was kinda cool. It made me see what kinda underwear she wore, and that just made me wanna tear her apart even more. I couldn't go home, 'cuz it was too far and it was too late; I was horny, had been teased, and now wanted some action.

So what did I do? The only thing I knew how to do: Go to sleep under the stars in the car, just like a homeless person. I slept there until the morning, but was still horny the next day.

The next day came and I went home. She called me that afternoon.

"So…did you like what you saw?" she asked. Wish I could've seen more.

"Don't know. Didn't see nothin," I shot back.

"Oh naw, but I think you did," she cooed. Just saying that got me ready.

"Well," I said. "You might just be right."

"That right? You wanna come back on Tuesday?" she asked. What a tease.

"For what?," I asked. "Just to check you out in the window again, knowing I can't touch you? Another peep show just to make me even hornier than I was?"

"No, it ain't gonna be like that, I promise," she said.. "Just come by again. And by the way, thanks again for last night. It was unusual, but I still enjoyed it."

"No problem. That's what I do: put smiles on women's faces."

"Okay, right. You gonna come or what?"

"Tuesday you say?"

"Yeah. I'm off that day. Come on over."

"Okay, I can do that. I'll come by."

"Okay!" she said. I could hear her grinning over the phone. "I'll see you Tuesday."

"Bet."

V.

Ahh...Terrific Tuesday! But Then There Was Kaci's Momma...

Tuesday came and I was THERE. During this time in my life, I worked under the iron glove of corporate America, a.k.a. The Machine. So being that I always felt like a slave to the system, I called in sick and took off, searchin' for my freedom. But I was livin' with the folks, so I had to make it look like I was off to work. I got up at the same time, got dressed, and was out. Only thing about this was how Kaci had forgotten to tell me that traffic out there was a trip in the morning, and how I was gonna run right into the thick of it on the way to her house.

So I left the crib about eight, and when I finally finished fighting against the traffic, it was about ten-fifteen, easy. Was it worth lyin' to my folks and my job in order to come see her? Absolutely!

When I finally got there, I thought we were gonna be alone. I rang the doorbell, and guess who answered? What every horny brotha fears about a chick who lives at home…her momma.
Dammit, Jim!

The day was already off to a bad start, and her momma being there only made things worse. Like mother like daughter, though. They had some STRONG genes and bore a striking resemblance to one another. Now I see who she got her grin from. Didn't know at the time but eventually found out that her mom was a Simpleton. She smiled at me all the time, and I didn't know if she was slow, psychotic or what.

"Yes?" her momma asked, holding the door and grinning ear-to-ear.

"Good morning, ma'am. I was wondering if Kaci was here?"

She paused, like coming over here in the morning was a crime or something. Then, "Yes she's here. And you are?"

"Al, ma'am."

She got offended when I said that. "Don't be callin' me no 'ma'am'. My momma was a ma'am. But I'm not. Kaci! Your friend's here!" she hollered out. Kaci didn't respond at first.

"KACI!!" she screamed out again.

"WHAT?!"

"Somebody named Al is here to see you!" Kaci's tone went from agitated to excited.

"Ohhhkayyyy!! Be right downnnn!!"

Her mom looked back at me. "She'll be right with you."

"Thanks. 'Preciate it."

I was still standing at the door. Her mom thought about it, and then spoke. "Oh, I'm sorry. Where are *my* manners? Would you like to come in?" she asked.

"Sure." Naw. I'd rather just stand there all day.

I went in and sat down on the couch. Her mom followed behind me, sat down next to me and just stared. Hard. I tried not to look, but you know how it is when you feel eyes burnin' a hole in your face. I looked directly at her again.

"Yes?" I asked. I noticed her clothes for the first time, and she had on a nurse's uniform. There was the smile again. I thought to myself, *Either this broad is happy all the time, or she's just plain mental. Maybe I need to get ready to run up outta here. She don't look like she can run, so I should be good.*

The whole "meetin' the mother" event was surreal, weird like one of those Twilight Zone episodes. But back to mom. She was still smiling, eyein' me up and down.

"Yes ma'am?"

Then out of nowhere "Can I take your blood pressure?" she asked. Hahaha, hilarious. What a freak! The comment caught me off-guard.

"What?" I asked.

"Do you mind if I take your blood pressure?" she asked again.

Okay, this broad was crazy. Even though she looked real good in that uniform (ass and everything), a lot of times, it's usually the fly ones that's crazy as hell, and she was no exception. What kind of person asks to take another person's blood pressure when they first meet 'em? I didn't know what to say, it was such an offbeat request. Still, what if I said the wrong thing? She might've tried to either cut me or strangle with the blood pressure machine. I didn't have a choice.

"I guess you can," was my response. She jumped all on my ass with that shit, whipping it out and quickly getting to business on my arm. While she was taking it, Kaci finally brought her ass down. She looked at her mom taking my pressure, and rolled her eyes.

"Ma, leave him alone! You gotta excuse her. She just got her nurse certification, and wants to try out her skills."

"One ten over sixty," her mom commented. "That's good. Good pressure." I looked at Kaci. Kaci just shook her head.

"I don't know what she's talkin' about, Al," Kaci said. "She's gone crazy over being a nurse."

"Ain't nothin' wrong with practicing out your skill, is it?," her mom yelled out. "That's how you get to be the best!" she continued.

"I guess not," I said, as she unhooked the machine, stood up, smoothed out her nurse's uniform, and then told Kaci, "Okay, I'm off to work."

"Okay, bye! Have a good first day!"

"I will!" she said, heading out the door.

How nice, I thought. *Mom supports daughter. Daughter's kinda supportive of mother.* Nice. Little did I know that that friendly exchange was just a front. I'd find out later just how off both of 'em were. Crazy is how crazy does.

No sooner had her mom left, Kaci was all over me. "Wow! You got dressed just to come over here?" she asked.

"Noooo… I got dressed because I told my folks I was headed to work."

"And you came to see me instead?"

"Hell yeah, I came to see you!" With that, she slid on top of me. Even kissed me on the cheek. "Mmmm, I like that."

She had on some stretch pants and a tee. She took my hand. "Come on."

Come on? "Where we goin'?" I asked.

"To a surprise."

"But I don't like surprises!"

"You're gonna like this one. Trust me. Now come on." She led the way upstairs to the first door on the left. Turns out it was her bedroom.

"Here's where I did my little dance for you. You like it?" I looked around. It was makeshift, with cheap pieces of furniture alongside each other, with no rhyme, pattern or reason to it. Nothing matched in that room. But you know how it is when you really ain't got no money and you doin' the best you can, so I got it.

"It's cool." Then I noticed the bed. "Wassup with the bed?"

"What you talkin' about?"

I walked over to it. She had different men's names and dates carved all over the headboard. "This. What's up with all these dudes' names? I see Derek, Antron, Winston, Giovanni, Lamontay, Renaldo, and it just keeps goin'. And then you got dates next to and underneath them. Wassup with that? You tryin' to keep records?"

"Wha'? Naw, I ain't tryin' to keep nothin'."

"And where you say you from again?"

"Augusta."

"Oh, okay. Go on."

"Where I'm from people don't do too much talkin', we just have sex. That's how we communicate...body language. Takes away from the boredom, and it feels good, too. So I used to have a lot of sex..."

"What's a lot?" I asked.

"Trust me...A LOT," she said. So anyway, me and my best friend would just carve men's names into our headboard every time we slept with somebody."

"So what were ya'll tryin' to do? Keep a track record?" I

looked at the headboard again. "Jesus, it's gotta be about fifteen, twenty names here."

"Well, yeah. Now that I think about it, in a way, we were keeping records."

"Hmmm…you think?" I asked so sarcastically, wide-eyeing her at the same time.

"Yeah, I know." She paused. Then, "You probably think I'm a ho' now, huh?"

"Oh, I don't know." I looked into her eyes. "Do YOU think you a ho'?"

"Hell naw! But other men who wanted me but couldn't get it thought I was. They tried to judge me, and didn't even know me! That was down there, *and* when I first moved up here. But that's the reason I gave you my number in the parking lot. I really hoped you were different. And now that I told you and showed you this, are YOU gonna try and judge me, too?" she asked, staring at me with those seductive half-Asian eyes of hers. Damn she was sexy. "Or are you gonna accept me, now that I've told you everything?"

Better not put my foot in my mouth with this one. I was so close to gettin' some, 'cuz I knew she liked me. I could tell it. Why else would she have grabbed Winky in the club and given me her number? Why would honey have given me that striptease from her window, and now I'm in her room, right where I wanted to be? I believe we all know the answer to this. Plain and simple, she wanted to try me out, and I did too. I wasn't ABOUT to mess this opportunity up!

"Naw, baby, I ain't gonna judge you," I continued. "What's in the past should stay in the past, 'cuz you can't go back and change it, can you?" She shook her head. I continued. "What you gotta do is live for today, 'cuz tomorrow ain't promised to nobody. NOBODY, ya hear?" I emphasized. "Ya feel me?"

"No," she said, unzipping my pants and gripping Winky, "But I'd like to feel this. Inside me, of course."

Show's over folks. You already know what time it is.

"Well hell, ain't nothin' to it but to do it," I said, unbuttoning my shirt and tie, and then taking off my pants. "So let's get to it!" I jumped on the bed.

"Hold on, I'll be right back," she said, disappearing into the hallway and then to the bathroom. I lay down on the bed and it creaked. Guess she had worn the shit outta those springs and slats. I was getting good and comfortable, still ready and hard as steel. When she came back, she was butt-naked and glistening head to toe with baby oil. Guess that's an Augusta country thang. Didn't matter. Winky was ready, me included. She came over and stood right next to me, and then turned around and around, modeling the goods.

"You like what you see?" Did I?

"Oh yes. Yes I do. Thank you. Thank you so much," I drooled. Kaci was fine. Like Two Live Crew fine. Big booty and cute face. The only thing that was a setback was her chest. It was so small, that she should've been vice president of the IBTC (Itty Bitty Titty Committee), but this other girl I used to date named Black was first and in my opinion, the president. Kaci had a little more than Black though. Black had mosquito bites on her chest. But all that didn't matter though, 'cuz for what she was lacking in front, she definitely made up in ass. Good to know that she'd been drinking her milk.

"Do you want this? You think you can handle it?" she asked, ass still turned to me and then bending over.

"I do. I really do. And if I can't, I sure as hell wanna try!"

That was her cue. She came and lay down on top of me, put Wink inside of her, and we went for broke. Kaci's rep held true to the other guys' names carved in the headboard. In bed she was the bomb. Since we were both young, we had that boundless energy, so we kept going and going 'til we were bathed in sweat. After my balls were drained, and she was satisfied umpteen times, we finally stopped, laying there on the bed next to each other. I wanted to go to sleep, but had to make it home. I got up and started putting on my clothes. She looked at me with curiosity.

"Where you goin'?"

"Home. I wanna see you later on tonight, though."

She propped her head up with her arm. "Why?"

"'Cuz, like you said…it's a surprise."

"Yeah, but I thought you didn't like surprises."

"I don't. I don't like gettin' 'em, but I like givin' em. So I'm gonna come by.

"What time?"

"Oh, probably 'round ten."

"Ten huh? I don't know. I gotta stay here with my brother till my mom gets home, but when she gets back, I'm good. We might have to say eleven, though."

"Eleven's good. I'll be here to pick you up then. Be ready."

"Don't worry, I will." We both got up.

"Okay, cool. I gotta go. Love ya, loved what we did today. Kiss?" I leaned back down to where she was, and she planted a juicy wet one on me. I headed back downstairs, and she followed, still naked. I kissed her one more time.

"Tonight?" I asked.

"Yes baby, tonight."

"Okey dokey, then. See you tonight." I kissed her again.

"Bye," she said, smiling and closing up the door. I was out.

VI.

If _ANY_thing Can Go Wrong (Murphy's Law in Effect!)

During my ride home, I made up my mind that I wanted that ass all to myself. All mine and all the time. At that time, I was in school in a film class, and I had borrowed film equipment (cameras, tripod, lighting) for a project, so I was gonna tell my folks that me and some of my other classmates were going on a night shoot, just to cover my bases and make my momma feel as if I was safe. In reality, I just got a room at a cheap hotel. Tonight was definitely the night, and I wanted to have her all to myself so that we could go nuts and take it to a higher level.

Everybody who's reading this, and have been there and done this, say "I" right now. It's a fact: no matter how good a plan you may have, something's bound to go wrong. That's why criminals get caught all the time…Murphy's Law. And wouldn't you know that Murphy's Law was in full effect tonight? I mean, FULL.

First came my mom in my face, pretending like she didn't know where I was headed to, after I TOLD her SEVERAL times. She came in the den where I was showering in that bathroom, just askin' questions. Not to mention she was dressed in late-night Black-Momma style: that raggedy gown and hair rollers, with those pink house shoes/slides on. When I came out the shower, she was sitting on the couch, eyeing me suspiciously.

"Okay, what, Ma? Why you lookin' at me like that?"

"Where you goin'?"

"On a night shoot. I told you this already."

"Night shoot? You with a gang or somethin'? Who you gon' shoot? Where'd you get a gun from?" She didn't understand. She was old school.

"What're you talkin' about?," I asked. "We're makin' a movie. That's the type of shooting I'm talkin' about."

Her eyes got wide and rolled up to her head as if the information I told her just sank in. "Ohhhhhhh! I thought you were goin' to literally shoot somebody or somethin', y'know? Bang! Bang! And all that."

I started getting a little annoyed. "No Ma. No bang bang. We're doin' a film for my film class. Matter of fact, I don't see why we gotta talk about this again. I've told you over and over about tonight. How come you don't remember this?"

She got up with an attitude. "'Scuse me then. I guess I hadn't thought about it."

My dad was also sitting there, but not paying attention to our conversation. He spoke after seein' my mom get upset.

"Weez?" he called out.

"What?"

"Where he say he was goin'?" Not this again.

"Pop, I'm right here. You can ask me." He ignored me.

"Say he goin' to do a movie with some people in his class."

"What are you, blind? Helloooo?! I'm right here! You can ask me!" I was right in his face, but he continued to ignore me. Why?

"At this time of the night?" my dad continued.

"Yeah, and ya'll makin' me late!," I shouted back. It was already nine-thirty. Ya'll know through previous reading that my dad was a trip, right?

"So what?" he asked.

"So what? I'm the one that has all the film equipment for everybody. So I need to go." The horndog was talkin' and Winky was starting to speak through me.

"Oh. Well, you'll be a'ight." I got up and started heading to my room.

"Gotta go, ya'll."

I went downstairs and started putting on my clothes. Why do parents always wanna talk at the most inopportune time? That pissed me off, 'cuz the hotel room at that time was around fifty dollars, and you know brothas didn't have no money, especially in college, when we were dead BROKE. But I was working, and had saved a few coins for a moment like this.

My folks didn't care, though. After all, they thought I was shooting a film. Didn't tell 'em 'bout the Love Fest that was about to go down. But boy if they knew...they wouldn't have never bought me a car. But the point was, I did have a car, so at least I had some sort of transportation. I finished dressing, grabbed my keys and was out, with my mom still asking questions even as I was pulling out the driveway. I just rolled up the window. I left, and she was still standing on the front porch, clutching her robe and still in those hair rollers and house shoes. Get back in that house, momma!

And as soon as that episode was over, there came another one. I was rushing, tryin' to get out there to Norcross when a cop pulled me over for speeding. He asked me why I was in such a rush and I told him the same lie that I told the folks. He didn't believe me, so he let me get out (under gun guard of course) and pop the trunk while he took a look in.

TAA-DAA!! All the equipment was there so he couldn't say nothin'. Evidence in full vision. I didn't argue with him, just gave him the information he requested. I wasn't even nervous. Cool as a cucumber, with zero attitude. You see, down here in Atlanta, when white cops sense attitudes from brothas, it's either gonna be a ticket or an arrest.   And I gave him no vocal ammunition, like "Why'd you pull me over…man?" Instead, I was just as polite, and then after he checked me out, know what he said?

"You know, I appreciate you for being so polite and well-mannered. A lot of times, when we pull your people over, they wanna fight, cuss, and carry on. But you people (*'You people???'*) have to realize that we're just doin' our jobs, tryin' to keep the community safe." Okay, that's some ol' 1965 racist shit. "Know what I mean…bro?" No I didn't, but at least he didn't give a ticket. So I played the game.

"Yes sir. Absolutely."

"Good." He walked back to his car and got in. "Good boy. Have a good night," he said, handing back my license. "And please…keep your speed down to a minimum. I know how you people like to race on the freeway, but this ain't flight school. Take care."

"Yes sir. Have a good night." Kiss my ass, you brain-dead hick.

He went on, and I got the hell on. By the time I got to Kaci's, I was thirty five minutes late. She was waiting outside. When she saw my car she ran back inside her house, only to emerge again with her keys, screaming to her mom, "Mom, I'm out!"

I knew this because I had the windows down. Her mom was screaming back to her, "Where you goin'?"

"Out!" she said, and slammed the door. She walked down the steps and got in the ride. She seemed like she was pissed the hell off.

"Hey."

"Hey." She was real short with me.

"Are you upset?"

She sighed. "It don't matter," she said, looking straight ahead. Let's just go, allright?"

"'Kay." I crunk up the car and that was the end of that.

We drove onwards to our destination. For the most part, we were both silent, but she ended up holding my hand, still looking straight ahead. I was occasionally checking her out from the right corner of my eye to make sure she was okay.

When we finally got to the hotel and pulled up, her eyes got wide, but she didn't say nothin'. I noticed her expression, trying to gauge how she felt about this, since we had known each other for only a minute.

"Anything wrong?" I asked.

"Nah. Ain't nothin' wrong."

"Didn't expect this, huh?"

"Not so early." So she DID expect me to get freaky with her eventually! I did sense a bit of hesitation, so I decided to give her a way out.

"Want me to take you home?" I asked.

"Hell, naw!" She got out of the car, walked around to my side and opened MY door. "We here," was all she said. Okay then! I just looked at her. Then,

"Got that right. Let's go."

I got out, took her by the hand, and we went up to the room. No sooner had we hit the door than it was on. She pushed me on the bed, kissing me and licking me in my ear. Yes, the ear is my SPOT.

"Take off your clothes," she whispered, getting up and makin' her way to the bathroom. And don't think I didn't comply. I stripped so fast and got up under the covers so quick I scared myself, I was so anxious. She came back out the bathroom fully clothed.

What the? I said to myself. She came over and got in the bed with me.

"Now, don't peek." Peek at what? She got in the bed with *all* her damn clothes on. I'm supposed to look at…what?

"Ohhhhhhkayyyyyy." She slid under the covers. *Now she's pulling a disappearing act.* "Where you goin' now?" I asked. Then I felt her presence. Then I understood.

"You wanna stay there for a while?" I asked her, panting.

"As long as it takes." And then she went back to work.

"I see." Boy, she could come visit my neighborhood anytime. Hell, she could take up permanent residence if she wanted to. Anyway, after she had me ready for action, she came up for air and to give me a kiss, and then slid out from between the sheets.

She turned the t.v. to the video channel. We watched them for awhile, and then I was like, "Ohhhkay. So what'cha gonna do now? I'm all ready for you to saddle up, but you not ready to ride yet? I mean, what's up?"

"Be patient." A slow jams video came on, and she got up. "This is what's up." As the slow jam came on, her clothes began to come off, piece by piece. When she got down to the draws, she stood in front of me.

"So what'cha think?" she asked. I just kept looking at her and that body. For a minute I was speechless, again struck dumb by the booty and the rest of her. She was absolutely amazing. Finally, I formed a sentence.

"I think that if God made anything finer than the Black woman, He's keeping that for himself!"

She started laughing. "It's true!," I said. "You know He is! Matter of fact, you know what?"

"What?," she asked.

"You should think about changing your name to Sho'Nuff, 'cuz you are fine, sho' damn 'nuff!" I said. Damn if I didn't sound ghetto, but at this point I didn't care. Wasn't nobody there but me, her, four walls, videos on the tube, a bed, and opportunity out the ass. There was that Cheshire Cat grin again. I patted the bed.

"Scoot yo fine ass over here."

"You so crazy."

"I know it." She came right over, and from there it was a wrap. We did it like there was no tomorrow, like the survival of humanity rested on our shoulders, the way her legs rested on mine. Boy, back then, I could really really go, 'cuz I know that we ended up doin' it 'bout five or six times that night. After we finished, I thought to myself, *My Lawd...this girl is incredible.* I was drifting off to sleep after the last time, when she shook me.

"Al?"

"Hmm?"

"Al, wake up!"

"Why? Wassup, girl?"

"It's four o'clock."

"So?"

"So, I've gotta be gettin' back home."

"Why? It's warm, we just fucked each other's brains out, and it's cold outside. Don't you wanna stay here 'til the morning?"

"Oh no, 'cuz I didn't tell my mom that I was stayin' out all night."

"You didn't? She'll be a'ight." I turned back over to finish my sleep. What'd I do that for? She literally rolled me out the bed, and I fell on the floor, stomach first. That shit first woke me up...and then pissed me the fuck off.

"Ow, dammit!! What the hell's the matter with you?" I asked, getting up off the floor.

She walked around to where I was. "Sorry, but I've gotta get home."

She walked to the bathroom and started getting herself ready, leaving me to get up and get back on the bed, looking up at the ceiling. *Ain't this a bitch?* I thought. *Almost busted by the cops, then spent almost sixty bucks on a hotel room to get me some, and now she's ready to go, and it's cold as hell outside. That's pretty shitty.*

But the sex had been good, so I figured I owed it to her to get her home. I got up and started getting ready. I looked over at the clock sittin' on the nightstand, and was blown away.

"Kaci, are you out of your mind?" I snapped. "It's damn near five in the morning! You can't wait two more hours?"

"What's the difference between now and two hours?," she asked, putting on her makeup again. "Not a damn thang. I told you I've gotta go."

"Well what am I supposed to do about the room? Check out is at noon."

"I don't care what you do with it. Take me home, and then you can come back and sleep."

Damn! I got up and put on my shoes. From that point on, I didn't say anything else that was worth talkin' about. Just the basics. You know...one word answers? We got in the car, and I was still half-asleep. She glared at me, actually mad that I got mad.

"What's wrong with you?" she asked.

"Nothin'."

"So why you ain't talkin'?"

"'Cuz…I just ain't. I'm just sleepy, that's all. Tired."

"Oh. Okay then."

We rode out. She didn't say nothin' else, and I didn't either. We drove back to her place in complete silence. When we finally got there, the sun was coming up. I pulled up to her building.

"Here we are," I said groggily.

"Thanks. I'll call you later."

She jumped out the car, ran up the stairs, waved, and then closed the door. And that's all she wrote folks. Just like that, she was gone.

I know it wouldn't seem like it, but after that incident, we got close. REAL close. It got to the point that her mom got scheduled to work late nights at the hospital. I remember when Kaci told me that, I jumped straight up in the air, just like that white guy in the old Toyota "What a Feeling" commercials. For those still living in the Stone Age and can't fathom why I did that, I'll say it in big letters…OP-POR-TU-NI-TY. Hello? Opportunity for some Kaci boo-tay. And it was, 'cuz we were both young and hot, with sex drives that would make a porn star blush. To my readers out there…ya'll know what time it was.

VII.

Fast Forward…

In the two and a half years that we went together, I was burnin' that gas, kickin' it at her place every (and I do mean every) night until morning. Even when her mom got fired and was there at night, I was there. But when her mom *was* working, she worked at night, and by the time I got off, Kaci would be at her job, and I'd head to the restaurant first to see her.

Every time I pulled up, she was always at the front door of the restaurant waiting for me, even if she had a customer. That's loyalty AND love for ya. By the time she got off and we got to the house, her brother would be knocked out, and we'd be either on the floor in the den by the t.v., with the blanket spread out underneath us, or up in her room, with her diggin' her nails into the headboard, scratchin' out the other brotha's names. Boy oh boy, that was one of the few times in my life that I felt I could just be wild and uninhibited and just do thangs to her, 'cuz she enjoyed my freaky explorations and nastiness, and I enjoyed her nastiness. That was what I called the perfect situation.

Sometimes though, the perfect situation had its drawbacks. Example: Her brother Ted would sometimes wake up and come downstairs to get something to eat out of the kitchen, and he'd see us going at it on the floor. I'd had a chance to talk with him on a few occasions, and he was cool. But you could tell that he had seen a lot in his young life, and he definitely had separation and anger issues with his mom and with Kaci. However, me coming over there every night to bang his sister's brains out probably didn't sit too well. Another piece of baggage that added damaged to his psyche, I'm sure. But we were all young, so I kinda overlooked it.

I think that being there every night kinda screwed with him a little bit mentally, seein' me going up to his sister's room to do her (I caught him peekin' in on more than one occasion, with jaw dropped). Kaci was aware of it too, 'cuz sometimes she'd look up and be like "Ted, get outta here!" and then he'd run into his room.

Poor kid was probably traumatized, because I tripped out on him seein' us, and that kinda bothered me. Here I was on one hand, this man, trying to be friendly, trying to lecture him like a big brother from time to time since he had issues as a young man, and then him seein' me as just another dude hittin' his sister up. I did feel guilty at times. But I never let that stop me, because God doesn't like quitters.

I figured he probably didn't know how to exactly cope with the situation and so he probably dealt with things the only way he knew how. Maybe he liked his sister in a Caligula kinda way. Maybe he was fascinated to see live sex in his house and jerked off thinking about it. I don't know. All I know is that after those few times he saw us, he decided to stay in his room when I came over, which eventually ended up being all the time.

We used to to go for broke every time I came over, 'cuz Momma was never at home. Not only did we take it to the den and in her room, but also to the stove, in the bathroom, on the floor of her mom's bedroom, and even on the stairs.

During the time we were together, she managed to pull me in. All in. How'd she do it? When we were dating, stretch pants were the style. She started me on that. She used to buy pairs of cheap ones, and then when I came over, she used to like for us to have extensive foreplay, and then have me rip 'em apart, from the crack on down.

Secretly, she might've wanted to carry out a fantasy of being raped, with me being the pursuer, which I did on more than one occasion. It even got to the point of her wanting me to tie her up with ropes and handcuffs, and then lightly spank her, or even choke her a little bit. You'd best believe that when she first told me that, I was like, "Goddamn, girl! You like that wild shit, huh?"

"Better believe it. I need you to whip me, humiliate me."

"Why?" I asked, confused.

"Don't know why. I just like it. Makes me horny." And without further adieu…I began whippin', biting, and choking that azz. Constantly. And she liked it. Really liked it.

So let's be real for a moment: How many brothers have had a situation like this actually happen to them in real life? Outside of watching and jacking off to porn, how many of my brothers out here have actually lived out this type of fantasy? I bet if I sent out a survey, the response would be not many. But hell, I lived out mine with the fullness'cuz SHE wanted it: unlimited kinkiness. It was incredible and mind-blowin' every (and I do mean EVERY) night for two and a half years.

We had also gotten into role-playing, with her dressin' up in lingerie and letting me be Uncle Luke from 2 Live Crew, dancing and stripping for me in her room, letting me humiliate her verbally when she didn't "bring me the money" and taking explicit pictures of her, Miami-mami style. Again, I must say that bein' with Kaci was one of the best sexual experiences I've ever had. Ever. Luke pictures ya'll…Luke.

Lookin' back, I realized that this was one of my first relationships with a chick who I first thought was out of my league, 'cuz she was pretty as hell. But I didn't care. She was sexy, adventurous, cute, fine, and best of all, found me attractive. Those factors right there brought it out of me to do my best. I mean, what more could a man ask for in a woman? I thought she was it, boy! Kaci, my ideal woman. After all, who wouldn't want a straight up, cute-ass freak in the bedroom? Lemme say this: any man who'd tell you any different is lyin'. I ask you as the reader again, what more could a man ask for? I had it all. A perfect TROPHY chick. When we went out, she turned heads. Dudes were always looking at her on the sly, and I KNOW they wanted to say something, but they didn't. She had that look, that walk, those outfits, and that smile. But in spite of that, she always remained loyal, holding my hand, kissing me in public, giving me attention, and making these fools wish they had a chick like this. I was good.

But relationships always have a beginning, a middle, and an end. And in the back of my mind, I knew that things were too good to last. Especially with all that lovin' I was getting. And just like that, things began to unravel like a bad weave.

VIII.

The Foolishness & the Fool (Yep! Kaci's Momma's at it <u>AGAIN</u>.)

The foolishness started when her mom got fired. So how do you get fired from being a nurse, you may ask? I'll tell ya: When you misread a patient's vitals and pronounce 'em dead, when they're still alive, and then try to pull the plug on 'em...*that's* how you get damn fired! Jesus, how dumb could you be? So when her mom got the axe, needless to say, it fucked up two things. The first was (you guessed it!) Mom became unemployed and stayed at home all damn day collecting that unemployment check, pouring over the want ads, and messing up me and Kacy's mating time.

The second thing was that since mom didn't have a job, the bills started pilin' up, so guess who the family started depending on? If you thought it was me, think again, player. It was Kaci. Pressure was on her to cover *everything* with that little fast-food job. Kaci had to work extra hours at the fast food joint, meaning that she was paying bills, rent, and food for the three of them on a regular basis. That meant she was stressed out, had no time to kick it with me...and I couldn't get no lovin' like I had been used to gettin'. All of that exploration and kinkiness had come to a standstill. I know that in itself that what happened in that apartment was hell to go through for Kaci, 'cuz the stress was on her shoulders, and I know that it was drainin' her, 'cuz she had her dreams of things she wanted to do. But she knew what she had to do, so she went to work.

Looking back, I suppose we *could* have gotten hotel rooms when I wanted some, but it would have been only me paying for that, and I just didn't have that kind of loot, 'cuz I would've tried to continue the tradition of hitting it every night. Plus, she wouldn't have been in the mood, knowing everything depended on her, I'm sure.

So my position was this: If *she* was goin' to be the only wage earner, then *she* needed to be the one to start calling the shots on some thangs, starting with letting me come over and get my mating time back. You know, once you get accustomed to a certain type of lifestyle, it's hard to go back, knowhuti'msayin'? Sure was for me. We had gone from makin' thangs happen every night to sometimes, maybe, and then, eventually, not. I told her that somethin' had to give. She agreed. But what could we do?

At the time, I had a nice job workin' as a temp with a certain department of the federal government. It was cool, payin' four to five hundred dollars a week. You couldn't beat that with a baseball bat at that time in my life. Single, livin' at home with no responsibilities, with just a few bills to pay is how I had it. So since she was my woman, and I could see she was strugglin', I decided to make a conscious financial effort to help her out, and I did.

I continued to pour out my services to her until her mom got another job, since there was no way in hell that the hospital was gonna let her come back after that stunt she pulled. She might make another wrong call, the person would sue, and then EVERYBODY would be out of business, with that person having that hospital named after them.

So I was giving Kaci about a hunnerd, hunnerd-fitty a week, to help make ends meet. But then her mom found about it and decided that she was gonna get greedy and hone in on what I was givin' in order to support *her* lifestyle.

"Got somethin' for me?" her mom would ask whenever I hit the door.

"Uh...no," was my response, thinkin' that she was jokin' or something. But this is what she'd use against me to try to convince her daughter that I was no good.

"Girl, what kind of man are *you* datin' that won't help your own mother?" she'd ask Kaci.

But I gotta give it to Kaci, she knew better. I was helping them stay afloat, and because of that, she would always defend me. She'd defend me while I was there, 'cuz her mom would never hold her tongue, and even whenI wasn't there, she was always in my corner. I guess she did it because either she was in love with me, or because of what we had between the sheets was so powerful. Either way, I was proud of her.

"He's a good man, Ma. And you should be grateful, 'cuz he's helping us when he really ain't got to. I can't do this shit by myself!"

"I disagree," her mom would say. "And I think he should contribute a little more. After all, he's fuckin' you, right? And in my house, too? Hell, I think he oughta be givin' us a whole lot more, since I'm cool with what ya'll been doin'."

From the sound of it...it sounded like she was trying to pimp her daughter. Ridiculous.

"Well, I'm sure he's doin' the best he can...just like I am," Kaci would say. "So you need to get off his back and mine too, okay?

Remember…*I'm* payin' the bills around here now, so technically, it's *my* place. So what you need to do is to look through the papers and find yourself a job. That's what *you* need to do." That shut her momma up for a long time, and also brought a smile to my face.

So after a few more weeks, Mom left things alone. But she was still tryin' to milk me, 'cuz she was one of those people who never caught a break in life, 'cuz she was so stupid. But when a break did come, she'd move too fast and throw caution to the wind, causing the opportunity to slip between her fingers.

Case in point: the nursing job. Okay?

IX.

Twisted HER-story

I didn't really describe it at first, but here's a little information about Kaci's mom. Mom was originally from the deep-down, countrified region of Georgia…Santa Claus, Georgia, to be exact. That's right, Santa Claus. She'd only been to the city (that's Augusta, ya'll) on a few occasions, and since she was damn near as close to a black bumpkin as you could get, she got taken advantage of a lot. While in Augusta, she met a young brotha (also from the country who was visiting) who was in the Armed Forces, fell in love with him, had Kaci and her brother, and then got married and divorced all in the span of three years. She was only fifteen when she got married, and then sixteen when Kaci was born. So Mom and Kaci are only like sixteen years apart, and sometimes her mom acted like a dim bulb, like she was the child and Kaci was the parent. Truth be told, they really acted like sisters.

Part of it I know was because she didn't have a chance to enjoy her teenage years, since she had her kids so young. The other part came from not being financially stable and grounded in one place with a steady job.

When men think about gettin' married, it's different. It's the woman who dreams all the time about having that nice house with the white picket fence, along with a good and faithful husband. All men think about is a clean and quiet home to come to, good sex, fly clothes, and a dope-ass ride. We ain't thinkin' too much about the 'Happily Ever After' fantasy. And I know that Kaci's mom's ex-husband didn't, especially bein' a serviceman. I mean, everybody knows that brothas in the service move around a lot, fool around a lot, get drunk, high, and also beat their significant other up a lot, because they have so much time on their hands and they get bored easily.

Being young didn't make it any easier. Mom had been through the wringer on that, but somewhere, somehow decided that she wanted something better. So she took Kaci and her new baby brother and moved up to Atlanta. It's not that Mom was simple; wait…yes she was. I just said she was a bumpkin, right?

Another thing that started to happen was that because her mom was trying so hard to pressure Kaci into telling me that she needed more money, Kaci actually started cussing her out on a daily basis. Part of that had to do with the stress of her having to be the sole breadwinner, while Mom had her hands out like cups, just begging. The other part that didn't help the situation was that instead of acting like a mother to Kaci and trying to provide some guidance, her mom tried to be more like a sister. So when Mom lost her job, Kaci took over Mom's role, thus becoming Mom -- and Ted not really knowing WHAT part of the family role he fit into.

Yeah, pretty much a dysfunctional family if ever I saw one, and my dumb-ass got unknowingly caught up in it.

Her mom was unemployed for what seemed like a long-ass time, and then finally…FINALLY got a job. But even with that, it still didn't take the stress off my girl. She'd have headaches to the point of not even wantin' to get down with the get down. And many times when we'd talk on the phone when I was at work and she was at home, she'd suddenly be like, "Hold on!" Then she would cover up the phone with her hand and then it'd be a serious catfight for about five, ten minutes. Finally, she'd come back, all calm and collected.

"You okay?" I'd ask.

"Yeah, I'm fine," she'd answer. "Just that bitch in there makes me SICK!"

Hearing her call her mom that made me cringe. Even though I wasn't crazy about Mom, she still didn't deserve that. "Ay, Kace," I said. "Don't call your momma that. It's disrespectful." Then she'd charge at me.

"What'chu say? Listen: don't *ever* tell me how to talk to that bitch, all right? 'Cuz you ain't in my position, and I ain't in the mood!" she snapped. Okay, it was the way she came at me that made me snap on her.

"Hey, you'd better slow your roll, girl! I didn't do shit to your ass," I said. "So don't be takin' it out on me. In case you haven't noticed, I've been tryin' to help, not hurt!"

She got quiet. Guess she was pouting or something. It got real quiet for a minute. Then,

"Hello?" I called out. Silence.

"HELLOOOO?" I called out again.

"I'm still here." She was pouting. I had to make her talk.

"Why you ain't sayin' nothin'?" I asked.

"'Cuz...I don't want to. Why YOU ain't sayin' nothin'?"

" I'm talkin'! Tryin' to calm you down."

"Boy, I am calm! You be calm!" Then she caught herself. "Fuck it. You comin' over tonight or what?"

"I would, but what about your mom?"

"Please. I run this. I ain't thinkin' 'bout her sorry ass right now. She ain't shit." There she went again.

"Girl, stop. You know you don't mean that shit. You just mad right now."

"I am, 'cuz she pissed me the fuck off and I can't stand it. That's why I need some dick tonight. So I'mma ask you again: Are you comin' or what?"

"Heyyy, if you need dick, I'll be there. Givin' you what you need."

"Yeah, a'ight. So I'll see you tonight, 'kay? Bring your A-Game to this bedroom!"

"Hey, you ain't gotta tell me but once."

And from that point on, that's how it went. Shit just became routine again. *The Eleven p.m. Booty Call* is what I christened what we were now doin'. During this time, I had gotten a brand new job, working in a bank, doin' some lockbox bs from four until midnight. I had the no-life schedule, 'cuz everything went on during those hours.

The good thing about it was that I had somewhere to look forward to go every night once I got off, and had someone to wake up to every morning. That was a good feelin' to have. The only bad thing about this? While I was working, the rest of society was partying and living life. I had no life, except for screwing Kaci.

It seemed that after that little turbulent period, things were actually getting back to the way they were when Mom was working at the hospital. But that couldn't be further from the truth. Instead of things gettin' better, they started goin' from bad to worse, starting with Leroy calling her up.

Now who was Leroy and what did he want? First and foremost, Leroy was Kaci's ex. He lived down in Augusta. I had seen a picture of him that he sent to her last year. He was a muscular pretty-boy, one of those dudes who probably knew he looked good and exploited it to women so that he could get in their pants.

I couldn't stand his ass, and I didn't even know him. But dude looked arrogant, with his washboard abs and muscular chest and arms, and she liked that. This fool had even sent her a picture of himself showin' him stretched out by one of those community pools in Augusta, all oiled up, with a handwritten caption at the bottom of the pic that read,"Thinkin' of U!"

Now brothas, if you had a good woman and wanted to remain exclusive with her, and then told her you wanted to only be with her, would you REALLY want to see a picture of their ex shown on the mantelpiece with a shrine built to them (scented candles, fake flowers, and pictures of them together)? I know I wouldn't. When I saw that shit, and found out who he was, eventually I made her take it all down. But that was a fight in itself.

One day after we finished our session, and she went to light the candles up, I just plain out asked her. "Kaci? Why you keep lightin' candles for this dude?"

"I ain't lightin' candles for him. These candles are scented. I'm lightin' 'em up in order to get the stank out."

"Okay, but they just happen to be around pictures of him. Why they got to be around his picture?"

"Al, look around you. Ain't no other place in here for me to put them."

And she was right. The whole damn room was crowded with knick-knacks and junk. Still I wanted her to take that 'Ode to Leroy' bullshit down.

"Okay, so why don't you take Leroy's pictures down and leave the candles?" I asked. "We've talked and talked about this shit, and you KNOW it agitates me. Still having his pics and making a shrine to him is disrespectin' me, 'cuz I'm the one that's supposed to be datin' you! And lest we may forget: I'M the one giving you money to help you pay bills, buy food and help your momma and Ted out! And you continue to disrespect and ignore me by leavin' that man's picture up! Why?!"

"Told you I was lighting them to get the stank out the room." Really? And she went and lit the candles again. I went over to it and blew 'em out. She got mad.

"What you do that for?" she screamed. "I ain't thinkin' about Leroy! Didn't I just say that I was gettin' the stank outta the room? Ain't nobody tryin' to disrespect you!"

"Yes you are," I continued. "And on the sly, too. So the next time I come over here and see that that shit is still up, I ain't gonna say nothin'. Just gonna rip up the whole goddamn thing and throw it in the trash can." She got in front of the shrine and crossed her arms.

"Uh, no. You ain't. It's my picture."

"I don't give a shit. He was your man in the past. THE PAST. In Augusta. But I'm your man NOW, am I not? I mean, tell me somethin' so I can know what to do!"

"What you mean 'so you can know what to do?'"

"So I can decide whether to stay or bounce or leave your ass!"

"You ain't goin' nowhere," she said. And said it with confidence.

What a bold-ass statement! After all we'd been through, it came out that she still really didn't know me. And what she didn't know is that I had no problems at all dropping women. Even women who looked like her.

"That right? Okay then, you want me to stay? Take the shrine down, then! That or I'ma do it for ya, and I won't be askin' any questions."

"So what you sayin'?"

"Hell, I think I said it. Either the shrine goes or I'm out the damn door."

"Fine." She paused. Then, "Don't forget to tell my mom and brother 'bye' on the way out."

WHAT? Is that what we were doin' now? I didn't say nothin', just looked at her. I was kinda in shock, seein' that she'd choose Leroy's shrine over me. I started toward the door, but she tried to block me.

"Move, Kaci."

"Where you goin'? I'm just kiddin'," she said. "Had you goin' for a minute, though, didn't I?" I didn't say anything, just stared. Then,

"Okay, okay. I'll take it down. You know you're my honey bear, Al."
Awww. Then she gave me a long make-up kiss. She had me right
there.

"Well, thank you baby."

"Just keep that dick comin'."

"No problem."

X.

Leroy: The Truth Finally Exposed.

After that, the shrine came down. But then the phone started ringin'. And ringin' all night long when I was there. My guess was that she and ol' boy had been conversatin' (is that even a word?) all this time, and when she saw that I was serious about getting ready to leave her, she got serious and probably finally told him that she had somebody up here, and that it was over. But he still couldn't take the hint and let go. I think that was the point when he started to become obsessed with her and decided that he was gonna try and change her mind by calling her up again.

Honestly, we could be "in the mix" around three thirty in the morning, and the phone would start ringing. And she didn't have an answering machine, so either it would just ring and ring, or her mother would answer it and bang on Kaci's door just to let her know it was for her. Then Kaci would get up, go to another room and talk anywhere from ten, twenty, to even thirty minutes. A couple of times, I tried to let it slide, thinkin' that she was tryin' to break it to him gently (let him down easy) that she didn't want him no more, but after the ninth or tenth time, I just couldn't take it. I had had enough.

So one night while we were gettin' busy, the phone started ringing again. And ringing. And ringing, until her mom banged on the door and hollered out, "Dammit, Kaci! You know damn well it's for you! I don't know why Leroy's still callin' you! Why ain't you told him you got a new man yet?"

Yeah, why is that? I pondered.

She got up from our lovefest to go and answer it while I laid there and waited. Waited for about ten minutes, then finally I made my move.

I put on my draws and jeans, and tiptoed silently to the room where I heard her voice. She was like, "Of course, I still think about you. You know I do. No, I can't send you any more pictures. I just can't." That was good, at least she respected me somewhat.

"Why I can't? Because I haven't taken any new ones."

Wait a minute…what? What the fuck did she just say? I stormed in there like a Forty Niners' blitz and grabbed the phone. It was *my* time, and he couldn't have her.

"Al, gimme the damn phone back!" she yelled. But I pushed her back.

"Get yo' ass back!" I yelled at her.

"Hello?" he yelled. "Fuck is goin' on, Kaci?"

"Yeah, Leroy? This is Al."

"Who?"

"Al, mu'fucka. Her new dude. The one that's been her man for awhile?" Can't believe she didn't tell him!

"Yeah, okay. What about you? She didn't mention you, so why should I give a fuck?"

"She should have. Why the fuck you keep callin' her? Matter of fact, why the fuck you keep callin' here night after night, disrespectin' me?"

"'Ay dude, I didn't know she had somebody new. She ain't said a damn word to me about nothin'. But had I known, then I woulda been left her alone, y'know?"

I was in shock. "So she didn't tell you she was with somebody else?"

"Hell naw! She ain't told me shit!"

I glared at Kaci. "Hold on." I cupped the phone. "Why the fuck didn't you tell this mu'fucka you had somebody else up here in the A?" She didn't say nothin'. I continued. "Kaci, why you tryin' to play me for stupid? Do I look fuckin' stupid to you?"

I was mad as hell, ready to kick her ass. She knew it too.

"Naw, I know you ain't stupid."

"Then why didn't you tell him?" My voice grew louder.

"Because I still don't know how I feel about him!" she yelled back.

Then that fool started screaming over the phone. "Ay! Ay!" I put my ear back on the phone.

"What, punk?!" I yelled back.

"Ay, man! Don't talk to her like that!" Dude was goin' nuts.

"What?!" I yelled back. "Lissen bitch, I'mma say this one time and one time only. Don't call this mu'fuckin' house no goddamn more, you understand? I'm here every night fuckin' her, and I do mean *every* night, so don't call here no more! You hear me, bitch?" I think I rattled him, threw him off, 'cuz he got real mad then.

"Ay player, who the hell you talkin' to?" he asked.

"Talkin' to you, bitch, and whoever else is on the fuckin' line! Now what?" I said. And I'd say it again if he challenged me.

Male testorone and who had the biggest dick were on the line.

"Ay bitch...I'll come up there and beat that ass!" That right there set me the fuck off.

"And I'll be waitin', hoe-ass!," I yelled. "Bring yo' country ass on up here so I can send you back with a city ass-whuppin', A-Town style, you backwoods, barefoot bama bitch! I want you to come up! Come on bitch! I'm waitin'!"

Then in the heat of the argument, Kaci decided to snatch the phone away from me.

"Calm the fuck down!," she shouted. She knew I was hot. She held the phone, breathed deeply, and then proceeded to speak to her boy. I sat down.

"Leroy, I've just made up my mind: Just don't call me no more, 'cuz I don't want you no more. Understand?"

I didn't hear what he said, but I can guess he was beggin' and pleadin' for Kaci not to cut him off. All I heard her sayin' was "Because...because. Because, I said so! I'm with Al now. That's how it has to be."

At that point I left the room. But I still overheard her whisper to him, "We'll talk about this later," when she thought I was out of earshot. But I definitely heard her. That bitch!

I ran back in there while she tried to continue running her game. I snatched the shit outta that phone. "Listen, Kaci. I don't know what kinda fuckin' game you tryin' to play with my head, but please believe that I ain't the one! The same goes for this hoe-ass mu'fucka on the phone! You can keep fuckin' around with this nigga if you want, but if you do, I don't want your yella ass callin' me no... goddamn... more! You hear me, bitch? Do that shit again, and I'm out. No money, no support. Not a damn thang!" She got quiet, but I could see the attitude and the anger in her eyes. No response.

"HELLO??? I'm talkin' to you!" I screamed.

"Yeah, I hear you," was all she said. I then turned the rest of my pissed-offness back to Leroy's punk-ass.

"And what about you, punk?" I said, venom in my voice.

"What about me, mu'fucka?"

"Ay, if you want her,at this point, you can have her, 'cuz I don't keep up with no triflin' ass women who wanna be players! So you can have her, bitch, 'cuz at this point, I don't give a fuck."

"Fuck you, punk mu'fucka!" he said, and hung the phone up on my ass. I tried to star sixty-nine him, but Kaci's phone had limited features. Forgot the family was broke. I tried to get his number from her, but she wouldn't give it to me.

I was mad as shit. Kaci knew it too, 'cuz I had turned red as fuckin' fire and she unconsciously started to edge back to a corner in her room, like I was gonna beat her ass or somethin'. Hmmm. Guess she'd had violent standoffs before in her past relationships. I'm sure it was because of stupid-ass situations like this.

Now I didn't do nothin', 'cuz I don't hit women. However, I *will* restrain a woman's ass in order to keep her from going off on me. Needless to say, I stared her ass down and started towards her until I got in her face. She tensed up, expecting me to jump on her, but I just stood there and spoke through clenched teeth.

"Lemme tell you one thang, and one thang only. Don't you ever… *ever* in your mu'fuckin' life try to play me. Ever. Else it's gonna be me kickin' your ass all over this goddamn apartment and then through the complex. You feel me?"

"Yes." She backed out of the corner and sat down. I think I scared her. Up to this point, she had never seen my dark side. But that player moment she had brought it out.

"You think I'm a fool?" I asked her.

"Unh-unh. Nope. Not at all."

"So then, you must've thought that I wasn't going to ever find out about ya boy, huh?"

"I didn't say that."

"Okay, so then exactly what are you sayin?" I was confused.

"I'm just sayin' that I'm sorry if I hurt you. I was wrong. I was wrong to do that to you, and if you forgive me, I promise that it'll never, ever happen again."

I looked at her. "It better not, 'cuz if it does, I'm cancelling your ass. And when *that* happens, don't even think about dialing my fuckin' number again, 'cuz I ain't with it. You feel me?"

"Yes, baby. I do." She got up, walked me out of the house and I went home. First time that I didn't spend the night. Thought I had fixed that, with the lyin' and all.

Hmph, to that I say. It was definitely gonna get worse before it got better. However, Leroy never came to town. Otherwise, he definitely would've got a two-piece served with these hands.

XI.

Bad Habits

Kaci had three things I found out about her later on in our relationship. First off, she had a terrible, god-awful habit of lyin'. Not just about one thing but about *every damn thang*. Second, she was a chickenhead who thought she could slay me with her looks, like she probably did with every man that came in contact with her. Finally, I found out she was a lush and a future weed-head with no higher aspirations than making a career at the fast food joint, getting money, and blowing a large portion of that on her habit, now that her momma was finally working. That was bad, 'cuz in trying to help her, I fell into the game and almost didn't come out alive to write this.

So let's talk about the lying. When I met her at the club, she told me she was 21, and I found out she was really 17. When I met her, it was a month before she turned 18, so I rode it out. I was twenty. I found out she had dropped out of high school as well. I overlooked all of this 'cuz she was fine and was a giving Again, it was all good until Brotha Leroy called. Then after that blew over, who she really was and what she was about was constantly being revealed, like a curtain being pulled away. In short, that world of trust that she built up with me soon started to crumble.

Case in point: I remember one time we were supposed to have been going out to the club. She told me that she didn't have any money to go, so I told her that I'd pay her way. She was like "Cool" and I went to pick her up in the ride. She hopped in and we were off. On the way to the club, I asked if she had everything she needed. "Of course," was the response. When we got there, we waited in line with the rest of the folk, and when it was our turn, she suddenly said that she didn't have her ID.

Talk about pissed! Had you been me, you would've been pissed as well, having to wait outside in the cold. Yes, by this time it was winter, and it had been one of the coldest in Georgia. So folks had on layers upon layers of clothes on the outside and then peeled all of that shit off once they got inside. Coat check made a killing that night.

Now I know that a lot of ya'll reading this are probably thinking that they wouldn't have been so angry at the situation. But I'm the type of person that if I'm comin' to get you/pick you up, you should be ready and have all of your stuff together! That's the *least* you could do for me.

I also hate it when I put forth the effort to get myself ready and be on time and my date is so nonchalant. I'm sorry, but that just ain't bein' responsible enough. Moreover, that's just plain damn lazy. I know that women have a lot more preparation to do than men when it comes to getting ready, but still…if I call you at one in the afternoon and we agree to do something, then dammit, by eight thirty that night, you should be ready to go.   Throughout our relationship, Kaci was never, ever, ever on time. She liked to piddle around until the very last minute, and then she'd finally go and get ready.

So now, we're at the club door, and she didn't have her ID. She kept fumblin' in her purse like she was lookin' for it, and was holdin' up the line. I let out a frustrated sigh.

"Let's go," was all I said. She didn't hesitate, just came along with me. Silently we walked to the car. We usually held hands, but not tonight. We just walked separately. I didn't even look at her ass, and I always looked at it. When we got to the ride, I just walked around to her side, unlocked her door and opened it up. And she didn't say a word…just got on in. I went back around to my side, got in, and crunk up the ride.

"Al," she began.

That just made me madder. Gas was high. "Kaci, for all purposes of us still bein' together, please don't say nothin' to me right now," was my reply. She kept quiet until I got her home. Forty five fuckin' minutes from the club to her house without a damn word uttered. When we pulled up to her apartment, she tried to talk to me again.

"I'm really sorry," she said.

"Didn't I tell you don't say nothin' to me?" I growled.

"Yeah."

"All right then. Maybe the next time you won't be rushin' and you could check to see if you have your ID. And then maybe we can have a conversation. But you made me put miles on the ride, and pushed gas outta my tank, and it was all for nothin'."

After that, she went silent. I didn't care. For the next hour, nobody moved. Not a word was passed between us. Not a single utterance. Then she decided to speak.

"Look Al, I said I was sorry. If you don't wanna accept my apology, then that's on you, but at least I did apologize, so fuck it."

Then she got her ass out the car, slammed the door, and left. I burned rubber out of the complex. Didn't even wait for her to get in the door. I was still pissed for having driven so far out the way and for nothin', and then she offered me that half-assed apology. I wasn't no sucker, and I aimed to prove it. To fix her, I didn't talk to her for three days. Then, when she saw I hadn't called, she called me on the fourth day of the standoff.

"You still pissed?" was the first question that came out her mouth. Not a 'hello' or a 'what's up?', just that. I was ready to tear into her, but I was on refrain and restrain.

"Not no more," I answered calmly. "I'm cool. Cool as a fuckin' cucumber."

"Good," she answered. "So when are we goin' out again?"

I was bein' stubborn at the time, but I didn't care. "Don't know. Depends on you."

"On me, huh? What about next weekend, then?"

I was silent, and then, "Yeah, next weekend's cool. You uh, gonna have everything before you leave the crib this time?"

"I'll be ready."

"You sure? I mean, I don't wanna go somewhere, and you don't have everything you need." I was being sarcastic, but serious as a heart attack.

"I'll be straight."

"Okay. About what time?" I asked.

"Don't know."

"You workin' Saturday?"

"Yeah, but I get off at six."

"What about eight, then? Eight good for ya?"

"Yeah, eight's good. You gonna be here on time?"

"Ain't I always on time?"

"Yeah, you are." She looked at me and then smiled.

"All right then."

"Damn, Al. You ain't gotta be so mean. I just asked you a question."

"I ain't bein' mean. And I just gave you an answer. I just don't wanna be inconvenienced again, that's all."

"Okay, all right, whatever. Just be here at eight."

"I will." And after that, I hung up the phone. *We'll see on Saturday,* I thought.

XII.

Just Got Played…

Saturday Night

This particular Saturday started out pretty good. I got to the house and lo and behold, she was ready, with clothes on and hair and makeup done. I made her check her purse for *everything*. She assured me that everything she needed was in her purse, including her ID. However, I knew we were in for a night because of that hoochie Magic City catsuit she decided to wear. Lemme tell ya, Kaci loved attention. And not just from me, but from any man she came into contact with. Later on, I'd find out why.

At any rate, that night she had on these damn lycra skin-tight cat pants, with the pink leopard print all over them and a little black sleeveless top. Damn, with all that on, all she needed was a tail to attach to those pants, sho'nuff. I mean, girl was fine, and the outfit took all the imagination away but damn sho' brought reality in.

When I got to her place and she came to the door with that outfit on, I was like, "Where the hell you think you're goin'?"

"With you! What? You don't like my outfit?"

"*I* like it! Love it! Love it for me, but not for the public!" Matter of fact, me and every other man who's gonna be at the club tonight are gonna love it! "I'ma need you to change!" I said.

"Oh baby, don't worry about it. I'm with *you*, and believe me, I ain't goin' nowhere."

"Like the Leroy incident, right? Tell me anything." I know that was a sucker punch to the guy, but I didn't like the way she tried to play me before.

"Oh, you'll see. Let's go."

We rolled on out.

The club was packed, with the line literally wrapped around the corner. Fortunately, my crew hung out here on the regular, and they happened to be in the middle of the line. So when they saw us, they let us jump, amidst the frustrated sighing and the "They can't jump no line!" shouts. Hey, all for one and one for all, I always say.

We stayed there awhile, just talkin' with the fellas, with me all the while checkin' them, 'cuz I could see them checkin' my girl on the sly. Yeah, I was definitely feeling insecure about that outfit. The bouncer at the door was all in it when he saw her. We were in the middle of the line, and he called her out.

"Catwoman! CATWOMAN!" Everybody was just lookin' around. "Yo, you in them pank leopard pants! Come up here!"

Kaci got out of line and started to head to the front. I grabbed her by the arm.

"Hey, don't just go up there and leave me."

"I'll be right back. I promise."

"Yeah. Right-right back." I rolled my eyes.

I let her go, and she went on up and started talkin' to that big ol' joker. In addition to her just chumping me off, I had to endure catcalls and comments regarding her ass when she was at the door. Next damn thing I knew, she had gone inside. When the crowd saw what had happened, they went crazy and started clowning me.

"Oooh, damn dawg, your girl got called out to go in!"

"And she left your ass, too!"

And the crew wasn't makin' things no better.

"Damn, she did that. How'd you even let that happen?"

"Shut the fuck up." They were pissing me off.

I was embarrassed and confused, all at the same time.

"Man, Al, she must know that dude, or be fuckin' with him or somethin'. I think you got played, playa."

I got mad. It was one thang for folk you didn't know to talk about you, 'cuz I didn't care about that, but it was another for your boys to talk about your ass. I mean, whose side are you on?

"Whatever. I'll see her red ass on the inside. Can't do nothin' but wait, y'know?" And the wait took another forty-five minutes. When I finally got inside and walked around, I found her sittin' at one of the bars while some other dude was buying her a drink. I saw her, but she damn sure didn't see me. She was just crackin' up laughin', havin' a good ol' time. Totally forgot she was with me. I walked up behind her and tapped her on the shoulder. Her expression went from sheer giddiness to an uh-oh expression. Then the other dude stood up. Like he was gonna do somethin'! Yeah, right.

"Who dis?" he asked, pointing at me. I looked at Kaci, waiting for an answer.

"Him? This is…this is…uh, this is my boyfriend," she stammered.

Damn right. He looked at her in amazement. "Boyfriend? You lyin' trick! You *just* told me that you weren't seein' nobody. You told me that you were here with your--"

I had had enough.

"Boyfriend," I said, finishing his statement. "Look chief, I think you might need to get the hell on."

"Fuck you talkin' to?" He walked over to me, and from there, it was a pissing contest.

"Talkin' to *you*, fool!," I said, sizing him up. He was a little taller than me, but he was in round shape. "Look at you," I said. "Now if we got to fightin', on the real, who you think would end up in the hospital?" That fool thought about it, and all of a sudden softened. I continued talkin' shit. "That's what I thought. Get the fuck outta here before I bust that ass."

Without any type of trouble, he just stood there, muttering shit under his breath. It was then when my crew saw what was happening, and all of 'em walked over to ol'boy. All six of 'em.

"We got a problem?" one of 'em asked him.

"Need some help?" asked another.

"I think you need to move on, homeboy. And quick."

Without another word, he saw the deck stack, and bounced. I sat down at the bar and ordered a drink. The crew continued to stand there until he was on the other side of the club. Kaci looked sheepish. She knew she was wrong. Didn't even speak up.

"You okay Al?" one of 'em asked.

"Yeah man, I'm straight." I looked at Kaci. "However, me and this broad right here are gonna have lots to talk about when we leave this camp. Lots. Believe that shit." She started to get up. "Sit yo ass down, girl." She plopped right on that seat, lookin' scared, like I was gonna embarrass her but I wasn't. The bartender came over.

"What can I get ya?"

"Jack and Coke, please," I said.

Kaci kept her mouth shut, from the time I ordered my drink to the time I finished it. I kept my eyes on her all the time, until she felt them burning in her face. She knew I was pissed. Couldn't even look me in the face. She just kept looking around at other people, looking everywhere except at me, while I kept up my stare, eyes rippin' into her ass. Finally she couldn't take it anymore. She looked at me and decided to come for me.

"What? What you want?" she screamed.

"Fuck you mean 'what I want'?" I played it cool, even as the music was pounding.

"What's your problem?" My problem? She got nerve.

"Oh, so now I got the problem. You got that shit twisted. The problem is is that you got your ass up in the club first, courtesy of that fat-ass bouncer that you probably fucked who let you in, while me and the crew are outside, with everybody in the line clownin' me for what you did. I'm still waitin' outside, finally get in here and then see some bitch-ass buyin' you a drink! You don't see anything wrong with this scenario?"

"He was just bein' nice. I don't even know him!"

"That's what I'm sayin'! You don't even know this mu'fucka, but you actin' like you wanna get to know him! And then he gon' try me! I wish he would've swung, 'cuz then it would've been me and crew stompin' the shit outta his ass!" She kind of chuckled.

"You think so?"

"What's so funny? Goddamn right we would have. He should've tried me, and then you would've seen him get his ass beat!" She shook her head.

"I can't deal with this right now," she said. She got up and started walking.

"Fuck you goin'?" I yelled out.

"To the bathroom, nigga! Is that all right with you?" Really?

"Fine. Long as you don't stop along the way to meet somebody else."

"Whatever. You ain't my daddy. I'm gone."

And with that, she left. I knew she was pissed 'cuz I screwed up her game, but I really didn't give a damn. She couldn't say one word, 'cuz she was busted. I knew from meeting her the very first time she might've been a player, and all she had to do was say 'no' when I asked for her number, but she didn't. She liked being with me, or so I thought. The next question was how long was this going to last before her interest waned and she went to the next man? From what I just saw, the thrill was already beginning to leave.

I pondered this as she came back over and sat down next to me. This time, she had a smile on her face. It's like she thought about it. Her personality had definitely changed.

"I'm sorry," she cooed, giving me a kiss on the cheek. "Forgive me?" she asked, looking into my eyes.

"This time," I said. "But don't you ever try and play me again. *Ever*, you understand?"

"Yes baby, I understand."

"Do you? 'Cuz it seems like we just keep havin' problems. Seems like if you really understood, we wouldn't be goin' through all these changes," I said, frustrated.

"You right. I'm tryin' to change, I really am. It's just hard. But I want to, 'cuz I still want us to be together."

"Well hell then, Kaci, make the change."

"I am." As if on cue, one of our favorite songs came on. "C'mon. Let's dance," she said.

She took my hand and we headed to the floor. As we started to shake it, I could visibly see that a lot of brothas' eyes were on her, partly because she was pretty and fine, and partly because of her outfit. But with those looks and that body, all people knew about her was the physical. It's just damn impossible to see what a person's really about until you actually talk and spend a lil' time with 'em. Had they known how she was, they would also have shared my idea of kickin' her ass and then cussin' her out. That includes ol' boy who was made to move on as well. But I'm sure he was still in there, still checking her out.

XIII.

From Bad to Worse

Cut to a few months later. We're still gettin' freaky, but now the arguments were becoming more frequent, and each time over more petty stuff. Where we once enjoyed each other to the fullest, now, I just think we were just there, occupying space.

I *think* we were still dating, but as the number of arguments increased, I wasn't sure. it was just like we were going through the motions. The sex was still good, but you could tell that things were starting to dissolve. Instead of enjoying each other from every aspect, we just became physical, a need to literally cum and go. And that's all it became. Alcohol and sex. The stuff that we did, it didn't seem right…'cuz all we did was argue, fuck, and fight.

The drinking definitely had influence. Yeah, we still drank so much that everywhere we went, by the time we got there we seemed to end up hanging on the doors, spending most of our time trying to get out of the car. We drank so much that one night I got pulled over by the Norcross po-po, and when the lady po asked me how fast I was going, I was so fucked up, I guesstimated seventy.

Her reply to this: "Step out of the car please."

I stepped out. Then she looked over at Kaci, who was just as equally tore up but somehow woke the fuck up and looked as attentive as ever, even though her eyes looked glassy as hell and were red and bucked.

"Ma'am, are you able to drive?" the officer asked.

"Unh-huh, yes. Yes I am. Why?" The officer looked over at me and pointed. I was wobbling.

"Because Captain D.U.I. here was only goin' forty-five, and he told me seventy. So in order for me to keep his butt out of jail, you have to drive. Can you?"

"I can try."

And with that, she moved over to the driver's seat. The officer took me by the arm and put me in the passenger seat. I just lay on the seat, mouth wide open. Impervious to everything. I just wanted to go to sleep.

"Sir, I don't wanna see you in Norcross again in this type of condition," she started. "If I do, I'm gonna lock you up for drunk driving and I'll have your license suspended for a year. Understand?"

"Yes, ma'am." I looked at her again. She was cute, too. Shoot, if Kaci wasn't there, I would've made a move on her that probably would've ended with me in the backseat of the squad car.

"Good." She pinched my cheek. "Cute though." I smiled. Hmmm...I *could* have made that move! She walked over to Kaci and leaned in the window. "Have a good night, ya'll" she said, and drove off.

We made it all the way to the house with Kaci driving. I guess you could call it woman's intuition that Kaci would have been better at this than me tonight, 'cuz I knew t that night, I would have barely made it or may have gotten us killed.

Or...that could have been one of the worse cases of female chauvinism I've ever seen and become involved in.

But then, things took a turn for the worse. I think it all started with the night of the hotel/liquor incident. Kaci and I were going to try something different than sleepin' together at her mom's apartment. It was due to the fact that her brother now kept busting up in the room when we were doing us. And finally, the main part was that we wanted something fresh and new, in different surroundings, so hence the hotel would do the trick

It started out well enough. I rented a room, set up the music for the night, and went to pick her up. When I finally got there, she was at the front door, running down the stairs, suitcase in hand.

"Hey, what's…"

"Let's go. Go! Go!" she said, opening up the door and jumping in.

I didn't know what was up, but the way she jumped in the car had a brotha scared, so we got the hell on. When we were out of there, I finally got up the nerve to talk.

"What is wrong with you?" I asked.

"Just 'cuz my mom got fired doesn't mean that she has to beg and take my whole check."

Now as previously stated (or I may not have said it), Kaci was a high school dropout who worked at a very well-known fast food chain. That meant that she didn't make any real money. And now she had to act as the breadwinner because of her mom making that stupid-ass mistake at the hospital. We thought we were out of the forest because her mom had landed another gig, but who knows what went wrong this time? Despite our issues, I truly sympathized with her.

"She got fired? Again? Damn, I'm sorry," I said. "So what'chu gonna do?"

"I don't know what she's gonna do," she said in exasperation. "But she needs to get her ass up and stop feelin' sorry for herself."

"I know that's right."

"And that's why I wanted to get the hell outta there. I need this. And you know what else?"

"What?" I asked.

"She was tryin' to get me to ask you for some money again. But I wasn't gonna do that to you. Fuck that. You've done enough as it is."

"Yeah, well I'm sure that she'll be on her feet again pretty soon."

"I hope the hell so. Damn! I really need a drink. Let's stop by a liquor store, 'cuz, I'm ready to get tore the fuck up."

"I'm with that." We rolled out, and about three miles from her place is where we made the stop. I handed her some money.

"What we want? Champale?" she asked.

"You know it."

"Pink or Golden?"

"Ummm…just get both."

She got out of the car, and started walking in.

"Ay!" I called to her. "What about ID?"

A smile went across her face. "I don't need it," she said.

Little did I know that she came to this liquor store all the time, so they knew her ass on a personal basis. Damn.

She wasn't in there but a minute when she came out with both of the fine liquers de malt. Since she had her bag in the backseat, I just popped the trunk and told her to put both of 'em back there. She went 'round the back and put 'em in, but I didn't hear the familiar clink of bottles lying down and rolling together. To tell you the truth, I didn't hear much of anything for awhile. Wondering what was up, I walked around the back, and lo and behold…Kaci was standing next to the trunk, just drainin' the bottle of Pink.

"Goddamn girl! You couldn't wait?"

"Hell naw. I told you I needed a drink."

"A'ight then, you have that drink. Just make sure that you screw that top back on tight before you lay it down. I don't want that shit leakin' out and stinkin' up my trunk."

"I gotcha."

I went back around the front and got in. About three minutes later, I heard the clink followed by the familiar slam of the trunk and then footsteps. She got in and closed the door. From how fast she drank it, I knew she had to have a buzz. And with that buzz, I knew that she might've been a little fuzzy on the memory.

"You *did* screw the cap back on, right?"

"Yeah, I did," she burped. "'Scuse me. I…I told you I would, didn't I?"

"You did," I answered. "But I just makin' sure. Can't be too careful with malt liquor, ya know?"

"Yeah, I know. But I told ya I screwed it on. So it's on there."

Next destination was the hotel. I went and checked us in and then we drove around to the room. We both couldn't wait. Sex is even more carefree when you're drunk, believe that. And I was gonna get just as fucked up as she was and tear that ass up! We walked up to the room, I unlocked the door and flung it open, and immediately pulled her inside and threw her on the bed. It was time to get wild…and I likes gettin' wild.

From the bed to the kitchen table to the dining room chair, it seemed like we were goin' for broke. Maybe it was because we were in an unfamiliar environment, but all I know is that it was good.

It was so good, in fact, that when we were in the chair, she leaned over to look down at me, and panted, "I think I done fell back in love with you!"

Naw, she was in love with Mr. Winky, that's all. But at this moment, I didn't care.

"Oh yeah? Me too, girl. Me too!" I smacked that ass, and she slapped my face. That shit was crazy.

"Really?"

"Hell yeah!!"

"Well then, tear it up, boy!"

"I'm tryin' my best!"

She moaned as I went deeper, and then just like that, she came. And when she came, I came. It felt like my balls had been de-juiced. But it felt so good. I picked her up, still inside of her and carried her to the bed, where we both unlocked from each other and lay there. Lay there for a long time. I thought we were making a comeback, it felt so good.

Finally we both got up and got dressed. I went to the door and she lay back down.

"Think I'll go and get the bags now," I said.

"You need any help?" she asked, still lying on the bed, half asleep.

"Naw, girl," I answered, buttoning my shirt. "I got this. I think I can handle two little overnight bags." I opened up the door.

"Don't forget the Champale," she called out as I was closing the door.

I walked out, got the bags, and then walked back in. Dropped the bags, went back to the trunk to get the libations, popped the trunk and then...

Fuck.

Pink Champale, the bottle that she had been drinkin' from, was all in the back of the muthafuckin' trunk and had soaked through the carpet. The whole trunk smelled like a cheap liquor cabinet.

I was PISSED. Didn't I tell that heifer to screw that cap back on before she put it back in the trunk? I *knew* I should've checked it before we headed out, but I just didn't listen to myself. Bet I'll listen now.

I gathered up both bottles, closed the trunk, took a deep breath and took my time in getting back in the room. I knocked on the door, and when Kaci answered, I was holding a bottle in each hand. Even though I was calm, she could still see the anger on my face, and that woke her up quick.

"Hell wrong with you?" she asked.

I walked in the room and set the bottles down on the dresser. "Didn't I..." I slowly began. "Didn't I? Yeah I think I did. I um, thought I asked you to screw the cap on the bottle tight."

"I did."

I picked up the empty bottle of Pink.

"What's this, then?"

She stared at it, then looked at me. "I don't know how this happened."

"You don't? Lemme show ya. I need you to come outside with me so you can see this for yourself."

"See what?"

"Just come on out and see."

She got off the bed and walked back outside with me. I popped the trunk again. She looked inside, took a whiff, and her eyes got big.

"You see and smell this?" I asked her. "It's because of you wanting to get your drink on that my trunk smells like this."

"Unh unh, Al. I put the cap back on. I swear I did."

"Naw, you thought you did."

"Damn, I'm sorry." She turned to go back into the room, but not without a smart-assed comment. "But you got a job," she added. "You should be able to pay somebody to get it cleaned out." She walked back over to the trunk. "Damn it stinks! Smells like alcohol, ass, and axle grease."

What?

"What the fuck you mean 'I should be able to pay somebody to get it cleaned out'?" I asked, glaring at her. "You the one that left that fuckin' bottle open. I ain't payin' for shit! Your ass is gonna pay for it!"

She laughed. "Shiiiit. No I ain't! I only make six hundred every two weeks, and I ain't gonna waste my money on cleanin' up some shit that don't belong to me! Fuck that!" And after that comment, you know she started back into the room?

I followed her ass. I've always made a point of two things. The first is never, ever, EVER hit a woman (unless of course she's tryin' to cause you bodily harm) and second, if the argument you're havin' is goin' to escalate and explode in public, then you take it, internalize it and save it for later, when there ain't but the two of you around. Ain't no need or use in being ghetto and raising hell so folks can watch you show your ass and then call the cops on you. I never have and never will operate like that.

But I guess I should've thought of that first when I started to get loud. But I found out later that the manager (who was white) had been checking us out all along; just watching to see if we were goin' to fuck up. And we did. So back to the situation.

There we were, arguing in the room, our voices getting louder and louder, until she finally screamed out, "Fuck it! Take me home then, since you wanna cry like a little bitch!"

She then started heading to the door…Like I was gonna take her home! I beat her to the door and managed to block it.

"Move out the way!" She tried to move me, but I wouldn't budge.

"You must be damn crazy!" I shouted. "You gonna stay here and listen to what I havta say!"

"Listen to what? I told you that I wasn't gonna pay for gettin' that shit out of your car! Hell, I thought we were gonna have a nice time by coming here. I even thought the love was coming back. But that ain't happening!" She put her hands on me again and tried to move me. "Get the fuck out the way and take me home!" she screamed, pushing and hitting.

I pushed her ass off of me. "You need to chill! Sit your drunk-ass down and calm the fuck down!"

"Don't be tellin' me what to do! You ain't my damn daddy!" Again with the Daddy thing.

"And I ain't tryin' to be," I said. "But you gon' calm down before we go anywhere!"

"Fuck it, I'll walk home!"

I grabbed her by the arm. "You ain't goin' nowhere!"

"Take your hands off me, mu'fucka!"

"Girl, calm the fuck down!" I guess it was the booze, but I never saw her like this. I moved from the front door and tried to get both of us to sit down on the couch. When we sat down, we were both freaking out pretty hard, but she had finally calmed down a little. Reluctantly, I asked, "Are you okay now?"

"Just let me go. I'm just gonna sleep on the couch. I don't want you to fuckin' touch me, fuck me or anything else, goddammit."

"Yeah, okay. That's cool. I ain't got no problem with that. I'm gonna let you go. So don't do nothin' crazy." We were both exhausted.

And then, more foolishness followed.

There was a knock at the door. "Who the fuck is it?" I yelled out.

"Hotel manager!" was the shouted response. "Open up!"

And no sooner did that man say that than Kaci jumped up like a spirit possessed.

"Help me!" she started screaming. "Help me! He's tryin' to kill me!"

"What?" I went towards the door. "Ain't nobody tryin' to--"

"HE'S TRYIN' TO KILL ME!!!" she screamed louder.

BOOM! went the door.

Inside rushed the manager and a police officer. The manager pulled Kaci toward the door and the officer grabbed me and threw my black ass against the wall.

"Stay back!" screamed the manager.

"But it's not…"

"Sir, you heard the manager," said the officer. "You need to stay back, or I'm gonna havta put you down."

Now that…that was a goddamn shame. The cop was a brotha. I tried to explain to him again. "Sir…"

"Hey…shut the fuck up! Don't say anything!" Why did the officer have to be so rude?

"But…" I tried to continue.

"Shut your fucking mouth!" he barked back.

The officer looked over at Kaci, who was over in the corner pretending to be all shook up. Oh yeah, baby girl could've won an

Oscar for all of that damn acting she was doing. The officer went towards her with the manager standing beside her.

"Ma'am, you okay?"

I looked at Kaci, who was now 'play shivering', like I had just kicked her ass.

"I don't know," she said.

What? If there was any time that this damn girl needed her ass kicked, then dammit, this was more than good enough for the time. The fuck she mean she didn't know?

"Ma'am, again…are you okay?" he asked.

"Do you need us to take care of this man for you?" the manager asked. Kaci stopped shivering just like that.

"Take care of him how?" she asked.

"Well, I could arrest him on charges of domestic violence."

WHAT??? I thought to myself. If this bitch gets me arrested, I swear I'll lose it. The police would just have to take me down, 'cuz ain't no way I'm goin' to jail for some bullshit, and no way in HELL was I going to tarnish my record. I had a job, and a good one at that. This chick worked fast food. Whose job mattered most?

I just glared at her. She gave me an icy cold glare right back. She knew right then and there that all it took was a couple of lies on her end and I'd be led out of there in handcuffs. I didn't pounce, but I knew that I'd probably snap. And my mother had told me to leave her ass alone after she met her in the first three months of our relationship.

"No," she replied. "No, he don't need to be arrested. We gonna try to work it out...ain't we Al?" It was clear that she had the upper hand. I had no choice but to lie and comply.

"Yeah. Sure." And that's all I said.

"You sure?" the manager asked. "'Cuz if he's botherin' you..."

"I'm sure. He ain't gon' bother me."

"Well good. However, ya'll can't stay here. Done caused too much drama," he said.

"But I've already paid for the room," I said.

"Yeah, well too bad. You've caused a whole lot of disturbance tonight, and some of the customers were at the desk tryin' to get a refund. In other words, they don't want ya'll here."

Ain't THAT a bitch?

"Well, we'll leave," I said. "Can I get my money back?"

"Oh no, absolutely not. I think that the money you paid was the least you could've done in return for making the other residents uncomfortable. So you and your girl need to pack up all of your shit and leave." The manager was not budging.

I turned to the officer, but he shrugged.

"What you want me to do?" he said. "You heard the man. Get your stuff and get out. Both of you."

"Officer, is that legal? Can he do this?" I asked.

"Hell yeah, he can do this. He's the manager." The manager pulled out a Ben Franklin and gave it to the officer. "And I support him one hundred percent," the officer continued. "You heard the man. Time to go!"

The officer stepped outside, while the manager kept talking shit.

"Ya'll need to be outta here in thirty minutes. If I come back and you're not gone I won't be Mister Nice Guy anymore. Ya'll gon' see a real nasty bastard come out, and I know ya'll don't want that now. Do ya?"

Naw, we didn't want that. The manager looked like a weasel.

"Besides," he added, "I will have not one but BOTH of ya'll arrested for causing a disruption, and I WILL file charges. Ya'll got that?"

Kaci, who had thought she was gonna escape punishment piped up. "Yeah, we got it. I just think that it's real jacked up that it got out of hand, got squashed and now we have to leave without gettin' our money back." Hmph. My money.

"Lady," the manager smiled, "In this case, you really ain't got a choice." He stared at us. "Ya'll have a good night, wherever ya'll go. I don't know, and really don't care."

As he turned around and walked out the door, we both gave his white ass the finger. I mouthed, 'Fuck you!' to him, and looked at Kaci. We both said nothing, and it seemed as if the silence would last forever. That is, until the manager decided to pop back in.

"Twenty eight minutes!" he yelled.

Damn, that mu'fucka pissed me off.

We started packing up to leave, still in silence. I didn't know who I was angrier with, Kaci or that redneck fool who called himself the manager or the officer. However, I knew that my blood pressure was sky-high right about now, and get this-I really don't get upset! I was ready to bust Kaci out, but I just didn't say nothin'.

But man, that drive to her house seemed like an eternity. I think that we finally realized what went down, but we both decided not to say anything. As I was cleaning out the trunk, she was getting her stuff, and still looking into the trunk, we ignored the hell outta each other. Afterward, she got in on her own (I damn sure wasn't gonna open the door for her ass), and I got in on my side. The only thing that made noise was the sound of the engine, the wind blowing through the window, and the radio playing some bullshit song I didn't know. Outside of that, we drove in silence. For seven miles.

When we finally arrived at her destination, I pulled up and she opened the door and got out. I didn't say a word-just popped the trunk and waited for her to get her shit out of my car.

She pulled out everything. But check this out: This girl decided to walk back around to my ride, lean down to eye level, and then utter out, "You know I could've had you arrested."

Okay.

"Really? Think so, huh?"

"Know so."

"Okay then. Think about this. Get the fuck off my ride, bitch."

She looked surprised, like I wasn't supposed to respond to what she just said. But she got up off my ride, and I got the fuck on. I looked out my rear-view mirror, and saw her givin' me the finger. I didn't give a damn. I played it back over and over in my head. Because of her not makin' sure that the top was on that damn bottle, we got kicked out the hotel and my black ass almost went to jail over her lyin' on me. That bitch had nerve.

Again, if that girl had been a man…boyyy! I didn't talk to Kaci for a month after that shit.

XIV.

Dirty White Bread

&

the Dropoff

After the hotel incident, things went from bad to worse between us. How so? The girl got her driver's license, and she bought a car. Saved up enough money from her fast food career and bought an '81 piece of shit Ford Tempo. Christ, an American car for God's sake! When she brought it to my place, it confirmed for me that most (but not all) women DO NOT know the first thing about buying a car. That's why they keep gettin' screwed over and why dealers make a mint off of taking advantage of them.

I was still livin' with my mom and dad when she pulled up in it one night. Even in the moonlight, I could tell it was dirty white (dirty AND white), and when she pulled up, I heard this gurgle come from its throat before it choked and finally died. The cutoff was followed by a loud-ass BANG! It sounded like someone shot the car or the car shot someone. Either way, that shit was loud.

She didn't even have to ring the doorbell; the car announced her presence.

"Is somebody shootin' out there?" my momma asked.

"Nope," I said, looking out the window. It's just Kaci." Damn!

"What? Did she bring a gun?"

"Nope. Somebody gave her a car."

"Oh, Lord!"

"And she's comin' down the driveway now."

"Have mercy!"

I opened the door just as she was going up the stars to the porch. She smiled, turned towards the car, and then looked back at me like she had the greatest thing since sliced bread. Dirty white bread.

"So, whaddah you think?" she asked.

I looked past her and stared at the Dirty Ghost. *It's a hunk of junk!* I wanted to say, but I didn't. Poor car actually looked like it was saying, '*Please God...don't crank me up again. Just leave me. Leave me here by the curb. Please.*' Truly it reminded me of a lot of brothas who never pay their child support: deadbeat and broke down. And it really was broken down. Nevertheless, I had to lie.

"Oh yeah. Nice." I walked up to it to inspect it. "Looks real nice on the outside." Again, dirty white with an on-again, off-again blue stripe goin' from the bumper to the fender. And then I got closer and looked on the inside. Dammit.

Ever seen a deadbeat, broke down, ghetto-ass car on the inside? You know the kind: carpet on the roof just hangin' down and drooping so you can't see who's in the back of your car? Nasty-ass cloth car seats that have been cut up and then been repaired with duct tape? Dashboard that don't match the color of the car or the seats? Car seats were gray, dash was red and upholstery was black. Damn.

"So umm...where'd you get this from?" I asked, still peering into it.

"Used car dealer. You like it?"

"Unh-huh. Especially the inside."

"Me too," she said, looking back in the inside. "It's different, ain't it?"

"You ain't lyin'."

"Yeah, well you know," she said, not even catchin' on that I was bein' sarcastic, "That's just cosmetic. I'll take care of it."

"Oh, okay."

She went around to her door, unlocked it, and then leaned over to the passenger side and unlocked mine. "Come on. Get in."

In this deathtrap? You gotta be kidding me. "Baby, this might not be a good idea," I said, looking all in.

"Get in!" she exclaimed, with all the fury of a woman that has yet to be taken seriously.

"Getting in."

I got inside, but I didn't wanna. Not inside that tank. But then I thought she might need me in case the car broke down and she was stranded. Ah yes, the dumb things we do while we're still young. It took four times for her to get the car crunk, which to me was a bad omen right there.

Meanwhile, my mom still had the door open, still lookin' out to see if I'd been shot, or better yet, wondering why we hadn't gone nowhere yet. When the car finally started up, I motioned for Momma to close the door. I know she was worried, but she closed it anyway.

We were off. As we were rolling, I couldn't help but to think about plotting revenge on the person who sold her this thing. The engine didn't hum, it gasped. I wondered how she had felt when she was able to close the deal. Judging how the car looked and rolled, I knew that Kaci couldn't have cared less. All she wanted was a car, and that's what she got.

"So," I said, turning to her, "You take your momma or anyone else wit'cha when you bought this?"

"Nah, I went by myself and I got it myself." I could tell. "And it was a deal, too. I only paid four-hundred down, and after that, I'm going to finance."

"Finance how much?" I could tell that they had taken her just because she was a woman.

"'Bout three hundred dollars for the next twenty four months," she added while we jumped on I-85 South, goin' downtown. Yeah, they had definitely taken her.

"Oh yeah? So you think you got a pretty good deal then?"

"Yeah. I'ma do double shifts so I'll have it paid off in no time."

"Oh. Ohhhhhhkayyyyyyy.."

I calculated the total amount in my head, and it came to a little more than seven thousand dollars. Now you KNOW that car wasn't worth a fourth of that. But hey, as mentioned before, who am I to say?

"I've gotta make a pit stop first," she said as we were on the highway. We got off at the West End exit and then went down the street to the projects next to the West End Mall.

"Girl, where we goin'?" I asked.

"Underground Atlanta," she stated. "But first, I'ma get a lil' taste of somethin' and pick up Vera."

That little "taste" (as she called it) meant that we were stopping at the classic liquor store right across the street from Morehouse College's football stadium. We called it "classic" because countless numbers of students around the AUC went there for years when they couldn't buy liquor or beer nowhere else. It was there that the party started every Friday or Saturday, usually right after classes. And don't even talk about homecoming.

So we pulled up and she had me go get her Boone's Farm Apple wine, along with Pink Champale (o.k., don't act like you don't know). I got back in and then we were off again to pick up her girl.

We rolled up on a back street to some apartments whose name has long been forgotten. You know how in some parts of your city you wouldn't dare visit a certain place because you've heard of its reputation or urban legend beforehand? My friends, where we were was definitely one of those places.

So we rolled up, and folks were sittin' out on their porches at ten o'clock at night. And other folks were lookin' and whisperin', "Who dat?", and heads were just turning, following the car. Finally, as with all urban neighborhoods, we saw people walking. Where in the world were they going this time of night?

This was our experience as we rolled up. As we parked, Kaci motioned to cut the engine. Shiiiiiiiiiiiiit. Not in this mu'fucka. I grabbed her hand as she tried that shit.

"Ay, don't turn this shit off. I got this. You just gone and get your girl."

She smiled. "Kay" was her answer.

She got out and walked down the steps that led to the apartment. I continued to look around, casing the area for any type of bullshit, and saw people still checking out the ride. Shit, you would've thought that the way Dirty White Bread looked, no one would have come up to that mu'fucka. But there's always an exception to the rule.

Man, the next thing you know, some crackhead was approaching, cruisin' up to the ride like some sort of shark. Approachin' MY window.

"'Ay, 'sup, homeboy?" he said in that project drawl. I was kinda scared. You never know what kinda bag folk like that come out of, 'cuz you never know what they want.

"What's up, man?" I asked.

He reached in his pocket, and I thought this fool was gonna come out with a gun to rob my ass. Instead, he pulled out a sackful of nickel bags and shook it in front of me.

"'Ay. Got dis weed right here, man. The good shit," he said, taking out a few samples. "Got a couple of nicks, no dimes. Wassup? You good?"

"Yeah, I'm good," I said, looking straight ahead, hoping to give him the hint to move his ass on. He was just oblivious to all this, still standing in front of me.

"You sure? 'Cuz if this ain't your bag, I got a lil' bit of coke that'll take that ass to the moon!"

I glared at him, givin' him my most fearsome look, but in truth I was sittin' there about to crap my drawers. Hell, after all, it's not like I come to places like this on the regular, y'know? And then there's the walking. How come in every community near a city bus line there's ALWAYS black folks walkin'? And at ALL times of the damn day and night?

This coupled with the fact that right now I've got a broke-down drug dealer who looks to be in his early forties, getting high off his own supply, offering me some shit I don't even get down with…damn, how much worse could it be? But I kept my composure.

"Naw man, I'm straight. You oughta be worried about Five-O. I could be Five-O."

"Five-O? Shiiiit. Five-O ain't gon' drive a piece of shit like this, I don't give a damn how undercover they is. Shit, whoever's drivin' this shit oughta be shot anyway."

Just as he finished that statement, Kaci walked out with her friend, Vera. Dopeboy took one look at Kaci, looked at me, and then asked, "Who is THAT?"

"The one who oughta be shot," I answered. He looked her up and down, then looked back at me.

"Man…that…that's you?" he asked, eating her up with the stare. I countered.

"Yeah, that's me!. And as far as the weed is concerned…"

"Hey, I ain't here to bother ya." He looked at Kaci again. "Ya'll have a lovely evening." He walked his triflin' black ass away, and I felt relieved.

"Who was that?" Kaci asked as she opened her door.

"Now how the hell should I know?," I asked. "I was just about to ask you," I said. "He LOOK like one of your people."

Then Vera spoke up. "Aw that ain't nobody but Low-Down, tryin' to make some quick money so he can get himself a six-pack. He ain't gon' do nothin'."

I stared at her. "Ain't gon' do nothin'? Low-Down just tried to sell me some weed and coke on the down-low, and then when he realized I wasn't buyin', decided to just hang out with me at the car, steady runnin' his mouth. And then he undressed my woman, head to toe with his eyes…but he ain't gon' do nothin'? Okay Vera…what are *you* talkin' about?"

I could've smacked her for makin' me respond to that last statement. Just 'cuz she lived there and knew those folks wouldn't have saved me from getting my ass kicked if things went left.

Before we go any further, let me clue you in about Vera. In every way, she's one of those original project chick, ghetto fabuloso as hell, with the mannerisms, the dragon nails and hair, the big juicy fruit butt, and the bright-colored clothing.

She was chocolate and cute as hell until she opened her mouth. She was one of those types of chicks who loved fast food, but if you took her to a real restaurant to eat, she'd probably eye the place up and down and tell you, "I ain't never been to no place like this before."

She was indeed a piece of work. And her and Kaci were good friends.

How in the hell did *that* happen?

So now we're out driving again, and Vera's just giving nothing but positive vibes to Kaci about the Dirty White Breadmobile. I'm sitting in the back, almost on bare springs, just listening to this foolishness. Apparently, Vera never had a car either.

We drove downtown to Peachtree Street, and from that point decided we were gonna cruise because it was summer and that was just the thing to do. So we're riding, cruising, and of course, there were the brothas who thought they were ballin', tryin' to get some attention from the honeys who thought they were ballin' as well. But you know, men don't care. We'll holla at a girl if she's cute and standing at the bus stop in the rain with a plastic bag wrapped around her head. It don't matter. And that's how it was tonight. As we cruised, brothas were hangin' all out of the car, tryin' to holla at Kaci and Vera, like totally disrespectin' me by talkin' mad shit.

"'Ay! 'Ay, Shawty…whassup? Whassup girl? Ay, you cute as hell! Who is that dude ridin' wit' ya'll? Who's boy is that in the back?" Those became the questions of the night by every dude that rode by or got stuck in traffic next to us. I know Kaci was lovin' it, but again, she knew I was back there, so she tried to play if off, even if she didn't mean it.

"Be coo. That's my boyfriend." And that's all she said.

They didn't care. They'd just look back at me and I'd give them the finger. Most of 'em just smiled and drove off, but some continued to get their flirt on, still disrespectin' me. Still tryin' to holler at Kaci. Couldn't care less about Vera. She was hood, and most of all, she wasn't mine. One dude got real "don't give a damn" attitude while we were cruisin.

"Man, fuck that dude!," he yelled out. "He look like he lame as hell! Ay Shawty, what you *need* to do is to hop your cute little ass over here and let'cha boy drive on home! Drop that zero and get with this hero! That's what you need to do! Oh yeah, and your friend can come too!"

Kaci would smile, nod, and drive on. Vera would wave or flip the bird to 'em. Whatever. They could say what they wanted, just as long as Kaci recognized who I was to her, still sitting in the backseat. They could call me a punk or whatever, but it was still me who was gettin' in those draws and nobody else. That's right. NO-BODY ELSE.

So we drove on amongst those who wanted to try and holler, and now we're stuck in holler traffic, jammed up. All of a sudden, I had this terrific urge to pee.

"Kaci," I said. "You think you can get out of this traffic for a little while and find me a bathroom? I gotta drain the monster."

Now to me, this sounded like a reasonable request, right? And had I been behind the driver's seat, I would've pulled out of traffic in order to find the girl somewhere to go had she needed to. However, keep in mind who I was dealing with here: A cute-ass chick who I kept having arguments and disagreements with 'cuz of her lies and flirts. Arguments which were currently ending very violently and publicly.

You think the girl found compassion for a brother in my condition? Hell naw.

"Pull over?" she said. "We're right in the middle of traffic. Why're you tryin' to fuck up my night?"

See how selfish she was? "Baby, I'm just sayin'…I really gotta go."

"You should've thought about that earlier when you started drinkin'."

Bitch! I thought. But I tried to stay calm, even in this crisis. Even though my bladder was ready to let it all go. "You're right. I didn't," I said. "But I really have to go now, so pull the car over. Else

I'm gonna pee all over this backseat." Vera made this face, and I could see Kaci's expression in the rear view mirror, just frowning.

"So why you really gotta go now?" Why was she asking me this? I was already in a tight. So I snapped on her, because it hurt so bad.

"Goddammit, Kaci! Why the fuck can't you just pull the car over? I said I really gotta go. Maybe it's because we were in Vera's neighborhood, which is totally unfamiliar to me. Then you go in the apartments to look for her, leaving me in the circle of hell and which I could've gotten shot. Then Lo the Dopeman comes up to the car to sell me some shit I don't want, and then decides hangs out with me and scares the shit outta me so the adrenaline is pumping. Then I've been drinking. However, all that nervous energy has turned into pee…so that's why I really gotta fucking go now. So why don'cha pull over before I turn this raggedy-ass car into a fuckin' toilet?"

And after all that explanation and lip service, you know what Kaci told me? Get this: "Well, we ain't gonna pull over, and you never should've been afraid of your own people anyway. They ain't gon' hurt you."

"Yeah, okay, whatever. But I still gotta pee and we're stuck in traffic, all 'cuz you wanna cruise. But you still don't wanna pull out and find a bathroom? Okay. I'ma remember that shit, believe that," I said, looking out the window and still sittin' on those raggedy-ass springs. "I want you to remember that for whenever this piece of shit breaks down and your ass gets stranded and have to call me."

She stopped the car and glared back at me, like she was gonna cut my head off or somethin'. "What'd you say about my car?"

"I didn't stutter, did I? It's…a…raggedy…piece of shit. A hunk of junk that some jackass car salesman sold your naïve ass just so he could get a commission and get over. And don't let me get started and talk about your drivin' skills, of which you have none. Look at you. You got both hands on the wheel, grippin' that shit like you know an accident's about to happen, and almost kept running up on the curb. What's up with that? You drive like you're blind and handicapped."

Believe you me, I knew I was pissin' her off, and at this point I wanted to. She was being really inconsiderate, all because she wanted to have a good time. Kaci got mad as hell and just decided she was gonna go off on me. Let her! That's what she got for not lettin' me pee. She pulled outta traffic (finally!) and pulled over to the side to let me have it.

"You know what?? Fuck you Al! Who are you? You ain't nothin' but a piece of shit yourself! You think you're better than me, just 'cuz you got a little job that pays a little bit more than mine? Or is it because you went to college? Is that the real reason why you think you're better?"

"Ay, I didn't say that. YOU said that. Get it right, bitch."

"Bitch?" Vera said, eyes opening wide. I ignored her.

"And now you gonna disrespect me in front of my friend?"

"I ain't disrespectin' you! Vera hear shit like this every day, so I'm sure it ain't nothin' new for her! What the fuck?"

"Nothin'. It's cool, Al. Tell you what…since you talkin' about me and I can't drive, I'm gonna find you a place to pee. You wanna take the wheel?"

"Hell, naw! I don't wanna take shit. You ain't gon blame me for when it breaks down and try and make me pay for it. For real though, you y need to take this car back, and then take me or somebody who knows about cars to a real dealership so you won't get fucked over again."

"Please. If I was gettin' fucked, it wasn't by him, and believe me, it won't be by you, either."

"Okay then. Just find me a place before I let this go on your back seat."

Without another word, Kaci whipped the car outta traffic, hit a sharp u-turn, and sped back down the street the other way to the North Avenue MARTA train station, right in the heart of Midtown, which was and still is a gay community in Atlanta. She pulled up to the curb and put her hazards on. I looked around and then stared at her in amazement.

"Girl, ain't no bathroom here," I said.

"I know."

"So what you expect me to do?" I asked. Somehow, I already knew the answer to this response.

"I really don't give a fuck what you do," she said. "All I know is you talked shit about me, my car, criticized my driving, and basically pissed me the fuck off. You're an asshole. So now you can get to steppin'. Ain't that right, Vera?" Vera nodded.

"Ummm-hmmm. Girl you were bein' too nice, 'cuz if I was you, I would've kicked him to the curb a long time ago." Shuddup, Vera. You don't even have a car.

I could've punched Vera in her mouth. But for now, fuck her. I was talkin' directly to Kaci.

"Baby girl, Vera's just lookin' for a soapbox to stand on, and I ain't thinkin' about her. Don't you fall into this trap of listenin' to that bullshit. It ain't gonna get you nowhere, and is just gonna make me madder in the end."

"Whatever. Get out." She was being mean. Didn't even look back at me.

"You must be sick," I said. I ain't goin' nowhere. Fuck you, Kaci. Take me home."

Kaci looked at me in her rear-view mirror with disbelief. "Fuck me? Naw, fuck you. You fixin' to get the fuck up out my car."

And then the girl jumped out of her car and started around to the back to open up my door. I locked it. At least I thought I did. But it was raggedy as hell, and in a raggedy ass ride like this, hardly anything ever works. She grabbed the door handle and yanked it wide open.

"That door don't work!" she yelled, and tried to grab me by the arm. "I said get out!"

I jerked her back, pullin' her into the backseat with me so we were face to face.

"Didn't I tell you I ain't gettin' out and that I wasn't goin' nowhere? I'll piss all over this mu'fuckin' back seat, and it won't make a difference in this raggedy ass ride!"

"No hell you won't!" she said, and jerked away, trying to hit, kick and scratch me, all at the same time.

I fought her off for a while, 'cuz as said before, I don't hit women. But my bladder was callin' me and my face now had some scratches on it. But still, while she was unleashin' her fury on me, I had thoughts on the brain about just beatin' her ass and showin' retribution later. And I also had gotten tired of her showing out for her girl, 'cuz Vera was just watching us go at it. She didn't say or do nothin'. But I grew tired, grabbed Kaci by her wrists and jerked her towards me again. I was furious.

"A'ight bitch, you done scratched up my face and I'm tired of fuckin' with you. I'ma get outta this car, but don't you ever in your fuckin' life call or deal with me again. You understand me, bitch?"

I let her go, and she slapped me. Hard. "Just get the fuck out!" she yelled.

"Well get the fuck off me, then!" I yelled back. She got her ass up, but not before slappin' me like a pimp again. Then she got up, waiting for me to exit.

Without saying another word, I got out, slammed the door and stepped on the curb next to the station. "Kaci," I began. But it was no use. Girlfriend went back to the driver's side and strapped up fast as hell.

"Kaci," I said again. "I know you hear me."

"What Al? Fuck you want?"

"How am I supposed to get home?"

"Don't know and don't care. You ain't got no change to ride the Marta, huh?"

"Nope," I said, walking up to her door.

"Well I don't either." And then she sped off.

I didn't have any change whatsoever to catch that train to get home. All I had was a twenty, and I literally had to beg people at the station for seventy-five cents so that I could get on the train. But I finally got enough people to help me.

As I paid my money, crossed over the turnstyle and caught the train, I was determined that things would definitely change between me and her, and from this night, possibly for the worst. One thing about it, I knew something was getting ready to happen, because every action causes a reaction. Little did I know that this event was setting the stage for the beginning of the end for us.

Oh yeah, and as soon as I got off at my station (Westlake), I was up the stairs and peeing in the parking lot. Bitch.

XV.

Worse. "Ex"-Mas. Ever.

I love Christmas. It's that time of the year that inspires and encourages folks all around to show goodwill towards each other. Even the meanest person who would always tell you to kiss their ass suddenly becomes nice and wishes goodwill. That always tripped me out. No matter what color you are, no matter what economic background you come from, no matter if you are saint or sinner, it's just something about that time of year that makes people a little nicer towards each other. It's also that time of year where it's nice to give and receive surprises…nice ones, too. And I like gifts, especially gettin' 'em.

It's that time of year where the element of the unexpected becomes expected, and is welcomed most of the time. However, that's not what happened to me. This year was going to be a horrible Christmas. Subconsciously, I knew it was coming, what with all of the problems Kaci and I continued to have.

After the car incident, I refused to talk to reach out to Kaci. I had made up my mind that enough was enough and that if need be, I was never going to talk to her sorry ass again.

But you know, it's funny how opposites attract and keep attracting. Truth be told, I hated the way Kaci treated me in the past, but it was the making up part that was off the fucking chain. In spite of that, the bottom line was that after the car incident, I wasn't speaking, wasn't calling, wasn't sendin' up smoke signals, and I didn't care. Kaci was dead wrong for putting me out and making me walk the track at the MARTA station for some change like a two dollar ho just so I could get home.

But I was wrong as well for talking about her car and her driving skills, so I'll take that. Still though, I felt that it wasn't enough reason to put me out. Afterwards, I played the sucker role again by eventually calling her, giving in and crawling back to her, with the idea that I was acting like the bigger person by tryin' to forgive her. But when you've got a young girl who don't know no better, because they've tried to be opportunists, they really don't understand kindness. And I knew that a lot of it was because she had missed a lot of kindness and opportunities that other girls her age may have had in their lives. In the time that I'd known her, she had to grow up really fast and assume household responsibilities. Therefore, she took it out on me and probably had some other problems in which she lashed out on other poor souls in her past.

Ya'll, I really tried to be the bigger person and called first during the month of December. That's right, I broke my vow, but it was only because of the laws of attraction, and even despite all of that mess that went on, I was still in love with her and I wanted her again, plain and simple. I was thinking with my head between my legs. Had I been thinking with the brain upstairs, I would've let that go and looked for new opportunities.

But from the first time I decided to be the bigger person, every time I called, I either got hung up on or cursed out, or her answering machine came on. This foolishness went on until the third week of December, about the time when I was just about to say fuck it, and not bother her again. Ever.

Then she called back. She was so damn nonchalant, I didn't know who she was.

"Hey!"

"Hey. Who's this?"

"Who's this? So now you don't know my voice no more?"

"Again: Who is this?"

"Who you think it is? Kaci."

"Kaci who?"

"Don't act."

"Okay. So Kaci…what you want?"

"Nothin' much."

"Well what you call for then?"

"I called to talk."

There was a long pause. Ohhhkayy. "Well, since you ain't talkin', I'ma go now."

"Wait, Al. I…I…I just wanted to say that I truly am sorry about everything."

Sure you are. "Everything like what?"

"You know. Leaving you at the train station, acting a fool at the hotel, cussin' you out and hanging up on you. You know, all of that."

"Okay, so why you callin' me now?" I asked.

"To apologize. No reason." Her casual approach got me steamed.

"Yes, reason. I think you callin' me is because it's so close to Christmas. But I ain't gon' be no sucker this time. You know what?

When you put me out on the street like a two dollar hoe, expecting me to get home when I didn't have any change, and then never calling me to make sure I got home safely, I lost all kinda respect for you. It was fucked up and you're fucked up for doin' that shit. So in reality, I really don't wanna talk to your ass."

"I just wanna apologize. I'm sorry." Ya'll, I know for a fact that it was not sincere. I snapped.

"Kaci, who you think you talkin' to? You sorry, all right. One of the sorriest women I know. And then when I was tryin' to be the bigger man, the more mature person in the relationship, you just ended up cussin' me out and hanging up on me. Knowhuti'msayin'?"

"Yeah I do. I know I was wrong, and I also know that I've been a bitch. I know too that right now, nothing I can do or say would make you believe that I'm sorry. But I am sorry."

"Yeah, I know you are. You sorry, all right. A sorry excuse for a girlfriend and a bad excuse for a good woman. But I guess you really ain't got nobody to blame for that…except for your momma." When I said that, there was a long moment of silence on her part. "Hello?" I said.

"I'm here." I could tell after that gut-punch she didn't wanna talk, but I guess she felt that she had to. "I'll take that because I guess I deserved that. But is there anything I can do to let you know that I'm true? And…I…do…mean…ANYTHING."

Anything, huh?

Next thing you know, I'm at her house, her mom's at work, and we're butt-naked on the bed, the floor just gettin' it in and gettin' carpet burns as well. Make-up sex is a mutha, but only feels good for a moment. Sooner or later, we'd be fighting again, but at this particular moment and time, I really didn't care. All that mattered was the moment. And still, the sex was good.

After that, things started to get better. But it only lasted for a moment, because fate once again threw a monkey wrench. Before, I was at her house every night and we really got our love on. Then mom got fired for misdiagnosing a patient where she worked at and pronounced him dead when he wasn't. Then she got hired and fired again for the second time. Now how stupid was that, and what did that tell you about her and her mom? C-R-A-Z-Y. The fruit really don't fall far from the tree, does it? But Kaci could keep a job. And when Mom lost her second job, Kaci got her one, working with her at the fast food restaurant. So now, here they were, struggling again.

Personally, I don't think her mom was wrapped quite tight anyway. After all, when I first met her, she didn't say, 'Hello' or anything. Remember, she just walked in and asked to take my blood pressure.

So things got a little hard again between me and Kaci because of that new pressure of never having enough money in her house. Where she was once apologetic and endearing, she became distant and mean as hell again. I know that she was going through issues, but I felt that I was just the soundboard she needed to go off on.

Later I found out that she started talking to her mom any sort of way again, and her mom would just accept it. Boy, the way she talked to her mom? I just know that if that had been my mom, Kaci would've either been dead or shopping for partials to replace the teeth my mom would've knocked out.

I guess it's two things: The way you were raised, and the case of older parents. Since Kaci and her mom were close in age, Mom tried to treat her more like a sister instead of a daughter. But in doing that, she raised a snake that would eventually bite her in the ass.

All that was said to let you know that we were having problems again, and it was magnified since Kaci had to be the breadwinner, since she had seniority over her mom at the job. But with her working so much and being under so much pressure, this pushed her away from me entirely.

Eager to try and be there for her, I took her to a movie on one of my off-days, trying to get her to simply talk to me. In the movie, we laughed, shared a tub of popcorn and a drink. But it was when we walked out of there that the breakdown between us began.

"You know what, Al? I had a dream," she began, as we were holding hands and walking to the car.

"What kind of damn dream?"

"Just a dream that we weren't together anymore."

What the fuck did she mean by that? Was she tryin' to leave me all of a sudden? My heart started pounding. "And how'd you feel about that?"

"Relieved," was the response.

What? On that note, I let her hand go and we just stood there in the parking lot, looking at each other.

"Relieved? Why?"

"I don't know. You know how sometimes people start to grow apart from each other?"

"Yeah?" We started walking to the car again.

"Well, I think it's beginning to happen on my end."

"Sooo…what you tryin' to say?" I asked, with a knot of fear welling up in my stomach.

"There's nothin' more to be said," she answered so casually. I felt numb. We walked the rest of the way to the car in silence.

She got in the car, but I stood by my door in shock. I was hurt. I felt like crying, but I wasn't gonna let her see me do that and give her the satisfaction. Instead, I composed myself and got in. We stared at each other for awhile again.

"Damn. Now you got me frustrated," I said. "We were just here in the movies having a good time, holdin' hands, laughin' and eatin' a big-ass tub of popcorn together. Now we get out of there and you tell me this? How long you been thinkin' about this?"

"For a long time. I just thought that things might get better, but they haven't. Plus, I'm under a lot of stress right now, having to support my family and all."

Instantly I turned to a desperate plea. "Hey, I feel ya girl, but I honestly thought that things were getting better. I mean, I know we've had some ups and downs, but at least we tried to talk. At least I did. But now you tellin' me this…I uh, I guess that it's not that important for you to work on it. Just lemme ask you somethin' and you just answer me honestly."

"What?"

"Do you or have you ever loved me?"

Do you know that girl looked directly into my eyes and said, "Al, to be perfectly honest, I don't think I've ever loved you. I've just been with you, having good times. Nothin' more, nothin' less. That's all."

Now THAT hurt. I was losin' her and I couldn't do a damn thing about it. I felt some anxiety welling up, moving up to my throat.

"Well if that's the case," I asked, "What should we do about it? Can't we try to work it out?"

"I don't know," she said, shrugging her shoulders. "It just depends."

"On what?"

Kaci didn't answer. I grabbed her hand, but she snatched it away. I grabbed her hand again and held it firmly.

"Hey…what does it depend on?"

She just stared at me with a dumb expression on her face. Then she spoke. "Didn't I just tell you that I didn't know? I don't know what to do."

"But damn, you just gon' leave me?"

"Al," she sighed, "Let's just take it one step at a time. After all, you know that if you really love someone or something really bad, you havta set it free and then see if it comes back."

"And if it does, then it's meant to be, right?" I asked.

"Exactly."

Heard this shit before. Yada, yada, yada.

"So do you wanna be set free?" I asked. She looked directly at me, but was silent. "Wait a minute, don't answer that," I said. "Let's just do like you were saying and go from here, 'cuz at this point, I ain't ready to just give up on us. I want to try and work it out, knowhuti'msayin? I love you, girl."

With that, I leaned over to kiss her in order to let her know that I meant business, and she turned her mouth away. All I got was cheek.

"What's wrong?" I asked.

"You know I've always thought that kissing was too personal," she said.

"Since when?"

"Since now. Remember, we're taking it slow."

I backed off, looking at her. She looked straight ahead. I put the key in the ignition and crunk it up.

"All right then," I said.

I was caught between a rock and a hard place. In an instant, our relationship had gone from eighty-five miles per hour to zero, with the tachometer still idling. I'm just glad she decided to keep the engine running, at least for now. Little did I know that she was getting ready to cut the damn engine off -- choking our relationship completely -- and then pull the key out so we wouldn't have a chance to restart it, no matter how much gas I gave it.

For awhile I played up the affection game, getting more involved with Kaci's feelings, concentrating less on the sexual part of us. Offering her mental and monetary support whenever she needed it; taking her out when it became too much for her at home.

By the time Christmas rolled around, I thought we had made significant progress. We were actually talking again, and laughing together as well. In fact, I thought we were doing so well that we were really getting to a point of discovering each other all over again, and I was really enjoying it to the fullest. I guess everything comes around full circle when it comes to relationships…

Or does it really?

I knew that Kaci was a HUGE Prince fan. She liked Prince so much that when it came to stressful situations, she would always quote a line from one of his songs. She liked his albums from Purple Rain on up, but hadn't really had the chance to hear Prince when he was up-and-coming. So I figured that for Christmas, I would get her some of his old albums as well as some of the new.

Cassette tapes were in at that time, and I had a friend who worked at a certain record store in Lenox Square Mall who gave me the generous hookup for next to nothing. So I got 'em all: Prince, Dirty Mind, Controversy, 1999, Purple Rain, Sign O' the Times, Around the World in a Day, and finally, LoveSexy.

I bought a nice little gift box and lined it with tissue paper and individually wrapped each tape. When Christmas came (this was our second Christmas together), I flew over to her house and couldn't wait for her to open her present. Last Christmas I was really good to her. I gave her two business suits for future job interviewing and a Dooney and Burke purse, because every girl needs to be made to feel good, and

I believed in her and wanted her to be somebody. She gave me some duck shoes that you wear in the rain.

Not a fair trade exactly, but I was aware of her economic hardship. This chapter should be a supporting factor for all women who may feel that higher education is not for them, and should encourage them to stay in school. I mean, even with the suits, overall clothes did not make the girl. Here it was a year later and the girl still worked at the same fast-food restaurant that she was trying to get away from. And now she was trying to leave me.

XVI.

The Breakup

Bright and early Christmas morning, I was at her house to give her my present. Everybody was up over there. When I gave it to her, and she opened it up and saw all the Prince tapes, her eyes lit up like two Tikki torches.

"Oh, Al, thank you!" she said, running and giving me a big fat, wet, juicy kiss on the lips and a sensual hug. Got a kiss this time.

She also grabbed Mr. Winky right in front of her momma and brother. Right thing to do, but bad timing. Her family members just stared.

"You're welcome. Let go whenever you feel like it."

She let it go. Winky wasn't mad, though.

"This is just what I need to get me up and going! I'ma play these at home..." Her mom rolled her eyes, but Kaci continued, eyes still shining. "And in the car, in the shower, in my bedroom...everywhere! Thank you so much, boo!!"

She gave me another big ol' smack on the lips. "I'll be right back," she said, and left the den. I looked at her momma and brother. They just smiled, so I smiled right back. She came running back with a box wrapped tight.

"For you," she said, handing it to me.

Since the box was big, I got excited. Was it something by Ralph Lauren? Perhaps some jeans? Some suspenders? A new Polo shirt or sweater? How about some shoes?

I tore open the paper and ripped up the box. And it was...some shoes. And some cheap ones at that. For all that don't know, cheap shoes make your feet hurt. Just looking at them was enough to squeeze my toes in anticipated pain.

"You like 'em?" she asked.

"Oh yeah, girl. Love 'em."

In reality, I hated 'em. Looked like bus driver shoes. And to add insult to injury, they were pleather. Who did I look like to her wearin' these cheap-ass shoes? MC Hammer?

"Well good," she said, "Because I almost got you these two Polo shirts (got-DAMN!), but I decided that you needed some shoes."

I didn't need these. But I guess she was workin' with what she had, in terms of income. So I appreciated that. But these shoes...

"Yes I did," I said, holding them up. "Thank you, I appreciate that."

"You can wear these to work AND to the club if you want! They're just that versatile!"

"Yes. I can. Thank you. Thank you so much." There was an odor coming from them that smelled like fish. I wasn't about to go anywhere or be caught dead in those fish shoes. Call it bougie, but I just couldn't do it.

I stayed for a little while longer, just to eat a bite or two, but I must admit that in terms of gift-giving, I felt cheated. Now I understand that we all sacrifice to give gifts and what-not (see O.Henry's *The Gift of the Magi* for reference), but I felt that she had not put in even a hint of sacrifice or effort in order to determine what I liked and what I wanted. Hell, if you were with me for damn near two years, shouldn't there be some inkling of knowing what I liked? But you go out and get me these Herman Munster/Boris Karloff pleather black cheap-ass bus-driver shoes? What in the world? I guess she didn't know me at all.

Don't get me wrong, I don't associate a gift with feelings or caring about a person, but come on now...pleather shoes? The only people I've seen that kick them shits on a regular basis were folks in the armed forces, people in a marching band, bus drivers, or dudes that wanted to be like Hammer. Everybody's got their own style, but these shoes were nowhere near mine.

When I got back to my mom's house, all of my relatives were there. The first thing my cousin Jeff asked was, "What'd she get you? Hope she got you somethin' good, all the money you be spendin' on her!" I hesitated. "What you waitin' for?," he continued. "Show us what she got you!"

With a heavy sigh, I pulled out the box and pulled out the shoes. All of my relatives, including my momma, my aunt, my cousins -- *everybody*, got quiet. Deathly quiet.

Finally my cousin Randy (the alkie who doesn't hold anything back) piped up with, "God-damn! What the hell is that shit?" Everybody started crackin' up laughin'. "Damn! Didn't ya'll talk about getting' presents beforehand?" he continued.

"I thought we did."

"Don't look like that to me. Look like she got you good."

And then my other cousin Jeff added, "You plannin' to join the Marines? 'Cuz those kicks are all we wear during formal times. But we wear the REAL leather shoes."

"Umph-umph-umph," my mom and aunt added in unison.

"I can't believe she did you like that," my Aunt Cammie said, half lit with a Schlitz in her hand. "But at least she thought about you."

"She sho' did," my mom said. "She thought very little. Last year you gave her not one, but two…TWO nice suits and a purse. What'd she give you? Some rubber ducky boots. And now this year…" she pointed to my shoes. "This year, it's some cheap patent leather shoes. They're not even leather! They're pleather! Al, you've got to start dating some higher quality women! Some go-getters! No more pathetic save cases!"

And with that, the whole house just busted out laughing again, leaving me red and embarrassed. Eventually I laughed about it too, but I thought to myself, *Is this what she really thought about me? That I'm only good enough for some cheap pleather shoes?*

I guess that's all she could afford, but what in the hell was I really gonna do with these? Then I thought of a solution: After Christmas, I'd take them right over to my old high school and give them to my band director to give to a student who might not have been able to afford shoes to march in. Either way, I was gonna get rid of 'em.

The next day, the shit hit the fan straight out the blue. Out of nowhere, Kaci called me and straight up told me that she didn't wanna be with me anymore. The conversation was short and to the point. It went like this:

"Hey Al, did you like your present?"

"Yeah. It was cool, thank you. I really appreciate it."

"Glad you liked it, because this is probably gon' be the last time you hear from me."

I was shocked. "What? Wait! Why…"

"Don't call me no more, 'cuz I don't want you no more."

"Wait, hold up…"

But she didn't. She simply hung up the phone, and just like that, it was over. I tried to call her back, but she just waited for me to say hello, after which she'd hang up again. I kept calling her back, but she took her phone off the hook so it stayed busy.

I tried to contact her for two hours straight, then finally gave up. I guess that in truth, I had kinda been waiting for this bomb to drop, I just didn't know exactly when. But now it hit and it was causing excessive damage to my psyche.

That way she did that messed me up, and got me depressed. I kept asking myself if I deserved this. I tried calling her back over the next four days, but each time it was either her brother or mother covering for her with the old, "She's busy," or "She ain't here" bullshit excuses. This covering went on for three months.

I couldn't sleep, couldn't eat, couldn't think clearly. How could I? She fucked me over. Gave me no reason, no time to ponder, no warning, NOTHING. It all ended so abruptly. To me, what went down was just like me being in a coma: I was there and could hear and see everything, but there wasn't anything I could do about it. The experience had numbed me, kept me in limbo. I was literally like a zombie, goin' from one day to the next.

Eventually over those three months, it did affect my job. During this time in my life, I was still working the three to midnight shift of lockbox operations at a bank. Usually, I was friendly towards my co-workers, but since that happened, I became withdrawn towards them. I wouldn't even eat during my lunch break; I couldn't. Instead, I'd just go to the phone, try to call her again and again, and she would do the same thing; hang up or take the phone off the hook so it stayed busy.

What a sad time in my life. I remember crying all the time and envisioning myself dead, so she would feel sorry for me. I found myself playing out that scenario all day, every day. But still, life had too much to offer for me to go down that road and never come back. When things like a breakup happen, you just want things to stop and go away.

My co-workers eventually said something about my withdrawn behavior, and even my manager (who was a SERIOUS bitch) allowed herself to feel some sort of compassion for me. So out of the goodness of her heart, she offered me two days off (with pay) for three weeks so I could try to get my mind right. While I appreciated it, I still thought to myself, *two days a week?* Who's gonna get right in two days? Don't know who she thought I was.

Each week during those two days at home, I slept a lot, and in time, a little of my appetite came back. I also had an epiphany about the situation: No matter what I did and how I felt, Kaci wasn't coming back. Also in that moment in time, I realized that Kaci might have been dating someone else all this time we were supposedly together.

Look at the facts: she lied about her age, so why wouldn't she lie to get another man while she was with me? The girl clearly had game: a cute face, redbone and a tight, round booty, so why wouldn't she seek other options? Hell, I wasn't really sure, but all I wanted to know was why.

With reality hitting me, I went back to work stronger and focused. Time does heal all wounds, and eventually during the fourth month of those events, I was strong enough to go on and accept what happened. I had gathered enough power due to talking with my momma, my sister, my aunt, my friends, and two of my co-workers who had managed to lift me off without tearing me down.

I still wasn't better, but I was finally coming to grips and beating that demon down. All I could think about was her, the good times we had, and the fact that now how she might be screwing somebody else. Once I started accepting it, I eventually went back to my old laughy, jokey self. But in the deepest recesses of my mind, I still found myself wanting to know why she did what she did. I felt like I would never know. After all, she was a woman, and women do the strangest things. I figured that I would never see her again, and since I wouldn't, I would never find out...

Or would I?

You know, why is it when you've given up, or seen that all hope is lost on something is when that something always picks the most inappropriate time to show its ugly head? I swear. Boy, if I had the answer to that, I'd be a millionaire. But back to how I was feeling.

At this point, I had gone through the hurt, and was recovering slowly. My heart was done with Kaci, and I accepted it. I had moved on and had totally thrown myself into my work when she called me on the cell. Just out of the damn blue the phone rang, and it was her.

"Hello?" I said.

"Hey Al, it's Kaci." A brotha's heart started racing. Just to hear her voice excited me, but also brought back painful memories I had of our ugly breakup. As a result, there was a very long and awkward pause. I couldn't answer.

"HELLOOO?" she tried again. I struggled to find my voice.

"Hey Kaci, how you doin'?"

"Fine."

"That's good, that's good."

"Listen, Al. I…"

"Look Kaci," I said cutting her off. "Is there something you want?"

"No. I just called to tell you that I missed you, and I just wanted to explain why I did what I did." Long pause on me again. I was trying to process this. Then, "Hello? You still there?" she asked.

"I'm here, and I'm intrigued. Go on."

"No, I can't explain everything over the phone. I'd rather talk to you face-to-face. So if possible, I'd like to meet." I could hear the sincerity, but it just didn't feel right. I was kinda hesitant, 'cuz remember, she hadn't talked to me for damn near four months, and then hits me out of the blue wanting to explain now? Kinda shady, ya'll.

"But why? Why now after all this time?" I asked.

"Because I was wrong, and I feel like I owe you an explanation. So if possible, I'd like to meet with you. Is that okay?"

"I don't know. What would your boyfriend say? I know you got a new one, 'cuz I know you don't like to be alone for long."

"Boyfriend? I ain't got no boyfriend. I just wanna see you, you hear me out, and then whatever happens happens, okay? Please?"

Again, there was another long-ass pause on my end. Something about this just didn't sit well with me. On one hand, I had finally begun to have peace in my life, convinced myself that she had flown away and put her out of my head. Yet here she was again, four months later, calling me out and asking me to make nice and meet with her so she could explain her actions. And on the other hand, I really wanted to find out why that had been done to me. Curiosity, hurt, and anger started to rise up in me, but I played it cool.

"Don't know," I said looking up at the ceiling in my room. "You've gotta give me some time to think about it, all the stuff you put me through." I started cutting my nails.

There was a pause with heavy sighing. Then, "How much time you think you need to think about it?"

"Why? You on a schedule where you just gotta see me?"

"Naw, it ain't like that at all. I guess I'm just, you know…anxious I wanna get it off of my soul."

"Really? Okay, well when I decide I'll let you know, okay?" Silence on her end. I think she didn't count on this response.

"Okay then." That was all she said.

I didn't even say goodbye, just hung up the phone. Man, that thang hurt me to the core, yet intrigued me that after so many months this girl was trying to come back into my life again, and that shit pissed me the fuck off.

I considered my options. Should I: One, play the sucker role and meet with the girl to see if she was really sincere in an open, secure area; Two, talk to her some more by phone to determine if she was serious, or three, just say fuck it, ignore her request and move on, actin' like she had passed away or had moved out of town?

Which one, which one? So many choices!

A week passed. I would go to work, and it would mull over in my mind what her real intentions were with wanting to see me. I would pull her pictures out and look at them, thinking mostly about the sex we used to have and then start to reach for the phone to call her. But each time I would stop. Since we had been together, we had also made an amateur porn tape. And by me missing her, I would also pull that out and watch us getting it on and I'd get my rocks off. Cleanup on aisle four right here. Then I'd get mad all over again, because I'd go back to thinkin' how dirty she did me when it came to us on Christmas day. But still I wanted to know in my heart why she did what she did, so I chose Option One and called her.

To this day I still don't know why I did it, but when I did do it, she sounded more anxious and eager hearing my voice than in the last two years. I mean, she actually sounded happy to hear from me.

"So, you've decided to meet with me?" was the first question that came out of her mouth.

"I did, I did," I answered. "But only in public, in an open space, with plenty of other people around."

"Oh. Well I was thinkin' more of an intimate place where it's not a lot of people."

"Like where?"

"My house."

"Why?"

"Because I feel more comfortable there."

"Kaci, I gotta tell ya. This whole thing just doesn't feel right to me. I'm a little suspicious that you called me outta the blue and now wanna talk to me about us breaking up. Hell, you might try and do somethin' to me."

She sighed. "Al, ain't nothin' gon' happen to you."

"How do I know that? I don't know what's going on in your mind over there. What if you've thought about killin' me once I got over there?"

Boy, truer words were never spoken.

"Killin' you?" she said. "Ain't nobody tryin' to do nothin' to you! Don't nobody even care about that! All I said is that I wanted to see you and then tell you why I did what I did. The only reason I said my house is because my car broke down, and I wouldn't have a way to meet you. So that's why I'm asking you to meet me at the house. MY house."

I hesitated. "What about your mom?"

"Her? Oh, she'll be at work."

"Work? She got another job?"

"Yeah, she did. So she won't be home to bother us or interfere."

"You sure?"

"*Yes*, Al. Now…when you comin'?"

"Well," I said, looking at my calendar, "I really can't say. What day is good for you?"

"This weekend I ain't gotta work," she said. "So why don't you come through Saturday night?"

"And all we gonna do is talk, right?"

"Didn't I just say that?"

I could tell she was gettin' irritated. But her tone kinda got me upset. "Hey, don't get smart with me. I won't come over, so you better watch your tone. Get it?"

"Yeah, I get it. I'm sorry. Didn't mean it."

"Hope not."

"So, you gon' come, right?" It was almost like she was begging me. Something was up. But I guessed that I'd find out what it was.

"Yes, Kaci. Yes. I'll be there around eight or nine. Which do you prefer?"

"Eight is good. But if you havta be late, no later than nine, please."

I was amazed. "Damn girl! What is it with you and time? Long as we've been together, you ain't NEVER been stressed enough for me to be on time since I've known you! What is up?"

"Ain't nothin' up! I just think that at some point and time, I've grown up enough to realize that it's important to be on time. Like with my job, I've learned how to be responsible, especially when they put me on a schedule. You snooze, you lose. Knowhuti'msayin'?"

"I guess." I looked at the clock. It was around four in the afternoon. "All right, okay, I'll be there around eight-ish."

"Ooh, I can't wait. Don't be late!"

"All right then."

I hung up the phone. I wouldn't hear any more from her until that night when she called me on the cell. That day, I fussed about my room and looked in my closet, looking for that right outfit to wear so that when I got in that confrontation with ol' girl, I hoped she'd be thrilled beyond the alphabet to see me looking so sharp. Then I could say, "See what you missed out on, girl? All this could've been yours!"

It took a bit of time, but after two and a half hours, I finally had it together: Brown houndstooth blazer with a cream merino sweater, with baggy blue jeans, and some brown bucs. Al was ready. Ready to roll out and see what she had to say.

Then E.J. called. He was one of the members of the crew and a close confidante.

He and I had started hanging out on Saturdays ever since Kaci decided she was gonna leave. Tonight was no different. There he was on the horn, trying to find out what we were gettin' into tonight.

"Whassup, fool?" he began.

"What up, E?" I shot back.

"A'ight. What's the haps for tonight?"

"Man, lemme tell you," I began. "You know Kaci, right?"

"Kaci? Unh huh. What about her?"

"And I told you about how we broke up? That she gave me my gift, then told me that she didn't wanna see me no more, right?"

"Unh-huh. Yeah, I remember."

"Check this shit out. After damn near four months of not being able to get in contact with her after that bullshit, the bitch finally calls and tells me that she wants to see me so she can explain her actions."

"Damn, that's fucked up. When?"

"Man, that shit happened about a week ago when I talked to her, but when I did, we set somethin' up and planned it for tonight."

"Okay. So…you goin'?"

"Yeah, I'm goin'. But the only reason I'm goin' through with this is because I just wanna know why she did what she did, knowhuti'msayin'?"

"Yeah, I feel ya. You probably wanna know, and then once you find out, you can get the hell on."

"Knowhutimean?"

"Yeah." Then I had an epiphany, something that was more than foolproof. "Ay, E," I said. "Why don't I just pick you up, and then after this we just roll out?"

"Oh…uh, yeah," he quipped. "Word. About what time you coming?"

I looked over at the clock on my nightstand. "Probably 'round six or seven."

E didn't have a car, but he had money for gas. "'Round six or seven? That's cool."

"A'ight then," I said. "See you around six. Be ready, fool."

"A'ight then. Late."

"Late."

I hung up the phone. Then my cousin Jeff called. Jeff's a cop and was also a captain in DeKalb County. We were pretty tight and hung out often, which is why he called me. But he rarely calls, so I just thought it was just a co-inky-dink. Unbeknownst to me, things were being set up so that God could work and bring everything to light.

"What up?" Jeff asked.

"Ain't nothin'. Whassup with you?" I asked.

"Chillin'.

"Okay."

Whassup with you for tonight?" he asked.

"Shit, nothin'. Me and my boy E.J. just gonna be hangin', right after I go over to Kaci's and..."

"Kaci?" he said, cutting me off. "Wasn't that that crazy bitch who dumped you after Christmas?"

"Unh-huh."

"And gave you those funky-smelling shoes?"

"Yup."

"And so why are you still fuckin' with her?" he asked. Jeff could be a little crude at times, but his heart was in the right place. After all, he cared about all of his family.

"'Cuz man, she called me out of the blue, 'cuz she wants to tell me why she did what she did."

He snorted and laughed. "Hell Al, you don't need to know that. Why you wanna know so bad?"

"Hey man, I just need to know in order to satisfy my soul and help close this chapter in my life."

Really, I did wanna know. But closing the chapter? I still might've wanted to do something else with her. Like fuck her still, but with no conscience. Just hit it and quit it.

"But if that's the case, why do you think she called and wants to talk to you now?" he continued.

"Don't know."

"Me neither," Jeff responded. "But I think I should come with you, you know, in case somethin' goes down."

"Like what?"

"Anything man. You know that she's crazy, just from the shoes. Just lemme roll with you, just to be safe. You plan on being there all night?"

"Not really. Just wanting to find out what happened and then I'll be out."

"Cool. Just pick me up at my house. I'll be ready."

"Gotcha."

"'Bout what time?" he asked.

"'Round six or seven."

"Cool. See you around that time."

XVII.

The Dope Boy & the Setup

So now I had two folks to pick up. I was ready. I had my clothes laid out. It was two o'clock then, and it was time for my nap. I took my clothes off of the bed, hung 'em up, and finally lay down.

I never use an alarm clock; I just naturally wake up at the time I set up in my head. So I got up, jumped in the shower, dried off, lotioned up, and put my clothes on. Keep in mind that I was still living with my mom, so when I headed towards the door, she stopped me to ask questions.

Have you ever noticed that when you're in an awful big-ass hurry trying to get somewhere, there are people or events that seem to slow you down purposefully? This was one of those times, but I didn't recognize at the time that the Man upstairs was slowing me down for a reason. But had I known then, I wouldn't have gone.

"Mr. Alexander, where are you going?"

My mom was definitely tripping, but I think she had a feeling about things when things were about to go horribly wrong.

"Out, Ma. Nowhere special." I moved towards the door.

"Don't look like nowhere special to me," she said. She eyed me up and down. "Hot date tonight?"

"Nah, Ma. Just me and E.J. and Jeff rollin' out. You know, squirrel and girl-chasin'."

I couldn't bear to tell her where I was REALLY goin'. Moms really don't like it when their sons have been done wrong. They take offense to it and then try to play defense so their sons won't get hurt again. But sometimes sons gotta take the hit.

"Okay. As long as you don't go girl chasin' over to that damn Kaci's house."

"Kaci?" My eyes got wide. "What made you pull that name outta the air?"

"Don't play stupid with me, boy. You know exactly who I'm talking about. If I were you, I wouldn't have anything else to do with that thang, especially after the way she treated you. Giving you a gift and then callin' you the next day, breakin' up with you over the phone. Who does that?"

"But see, that's the thing Ma. You ain't me."

"Fair enough. So are you going over there in your girl-chasin'?"

"Ma, I said we were just goin' girl-chasin'. Did I say I was goin' to see her?"

"Naw, but you'd really be a fool to," she added.

"I ain't goin' over there, Ma. Get over it." I looked at my watch. "Matter of fact, I'm out." I walked out to my car, got in, and got the hell on.

I drove over and picked up E.J. at his house, and then we headed over to Jeff's in Decatur. At the time, I lived in downtown Atlanta, and E.J. lived in the boonies, off of Camp Creek in East Point. So I drove there first, and then we headed to Jeff's house.

Keep in mind that Kaci lived in Norcross, so all in all, I must have driven about seventy miles one way that night. I had a little, itty-bitty Toyota Paseo at the time, and it was damn near a roadster, so you know when I picked up those two, the fit in there was tiiight. Even though all three of us were some short brothas, it was still tight inside.

Jeff rode up front since he was my cousin, and E.J., since he wasn't able to stretch his legs out in the back by sitting, simply put his legs on the back seat and made himself comfortable. And this is how we rolled.

We didn't say too much as we were riding out, and that was because everyone who was with me knew what my mission was. I guess that they were just quiet out of respect for what I was trying to do, or they just didn't know what to say. Hell, I didn't know what to do or say either. So many things were running through my mind at this point, I just didn't feel like addressing or acknowledging them. Instead we listened to a couple of mix CD's that I made in order to take off the edge.

After the first one, I couldn't take it any longer, and decided to break the silence.

"So, it's still early," I said. Looking at my watch. "Do we wanna do something first before we go over there?"

Jeff didn't say nothin', just reached in his pocket and pulled out his cigarette pack. He tapped it a couple of times, pulled out a cigarette, and then lit it. "I could use a beer," he finally said.

"Me too. A brew or a couple of brews sound good to me," E chimed in.

"And some chicken wings, too," I added. "So again...where ya'll wanna go?"

"Let's go to Dugan's," J said, flicking ashes out of the window.

"Which one?" I said.

"Um, since we're already in the Deck (Decatur, GA), why not go to the one on Memorial Drive? It's close."

"You right. Let's go there," E chimed in.

"Yeah, dude. Let's roll up there, have a couple of beers, some wings, and then roll over to your girl's house," Jeff said. "Is that cool?"

"Yeah, that's straight with me," I said. "Dugan's on Memorial it is."

For all that don't know, Dugan's is a very famous bar that's been in Atlanta and heavily populated by Black Atllanta forever and a day. If you live in Atlanta, you'd have had to go to at least one of the locations. Either on Memorial Drive or the one on Ponce.

But the most heavily populated was the one on Ponce de Leon, where everybody and their momma goes. It doesn't have the best drinks, the best wings, the cheapest beers, or the best-looking waitresses, but it was one of those types of white establishments that Black Atlanta heavily hung out at and gave their business to with fervor. If you wanted to be seen, you were there. And there we were, part of that scene, out in Decatur, just sittin' at the table, having a few beers and wings. The game was on, the ladies were strollin' about, and the mood was on chill mode.

"So man," Jeff said, takin' a sip out of his glass, "Why you still fuckin' with that loser bitch?"

"What you mean?" I asked.

"I mean, it's that hard for you to find another woman in Atlanta? If it is, look around you! Plenty right here to choose from!"

"Yeah," E chimed in. "The ratio of women to men here in the A alone is about eight to one."

"What?" I exclaimed. "Who told you that bullshit?"

"Read Ebony, playboy. Ebony Magazine tells you everything goin' on in the black community."

E. J. was the type of dude that was always fact-finding. Matter of fact, you could call him the Black Cliff Clavin (you know, from Cheers? The guy who swore he knew everything, yet had a lock on nothing?). For what it was worth, I guess he was right.

"Oh, okay. So I guess Ebony just drops the stats and you read and plug into it, right?" I asked.

"Naw, he ain't sayin' that," said Jeff. "He's sayin' that basically with all of these women out here, why's it so hard for you to let go of this one and just get another?"

Jeff was already a womanizer. Yet I'm getting advice from this man? Okay then..

"If I were you, I'd have another," he said. "Shiit, I ain't you, and I still got me someone on the side. Matter of fact, I got me a stable my wife don't even know about!"

"No shit," I said.

"Man, trust me. It ain't worth just having one," he continued. "You've got to get back out there, explore other possibilities. Make that shit happen. Boy, lemme tell ya: I done had so many women that if I died today I could honestly say that I didn't miss nothin', when it comes to booty. Got all the ass I wanted."

"I feel ya," I said, taking a swig of my beer.

"So after we deal with this, and you find out what you wanna hear, you move on. Understand?"

"I gotcha. After tonight, you ain't gonna hear shit else from me."

"Well, good," Jeff said. "'Cuz I'm tired of your punk-ass cryin' over this girl. You sound like a little girl." E.J. laughed. I took another swig and gave him the finger.

"Okay, whatever. I know it's hard for you to understand, 'cuz you ain't never been in love, not even with your wife, now have you?" I asked.

"Yeah, well, my wife's an asset. And her and my children are basically my tax write-offs."

Damn, Jeff was cold, even by my standards. "Tax write offs? Damn J…you cold as hell."

"Hell, it's true," he continued. "And I'm just being honest."

"A'ight then." By this time, the waitress came around again.

"What else can I get for ya'll strappin' young men?"

"You can get us another round," J said, pulling out his wallet and tipping the waitress.

She took it, looked at the amount he gave her, and was like, "I'll be right back." Then my pager went off. It was on vibrate, so when I took it off my hip and looked at it, it was you know who.

E.J. was the first to notice it, and spoke. "Who was it?" he asked.

"Aw man, you know who it is…it was Kaci."

"What Shawty want?"

"Probably wants to know where I am and what-not. Be all right, though."

"Yeah. Better not keep her waiting," Jeff said, tipping his glass to put salt in his beer. "You know how much you're dying to see her and hear that little bullshit explanation."

"Hell, she can wait," I said. "She made me wait for four months without hearing from her, so she'll be all right."

The waitress came back with another pitcher. We drained it and then E.J. bought another one. By now, we were faded and working on that third pitcher that the waitress just brought over to the table. I was sleepy, had a nice buzz, and my face felt numb. But we kept drinking, determined to put that last pitcher away.

I looked over at Jeff and his eyes were rolling to the back of his head. I looked over at E.J. and his head was bobbing to some music that no one else in the bar was hearing because some football game was on.

Yeah, we were faded, fucked up, whatever. But still, that shit felt so good.

"Another pitcher?" the waitress asked, coming over and gathering our already drained third pitcher. When no one answered she was like, "HELLOOOO? Ya'll need any more pitchers?"

"Nah," I finally piped up. "We're good."

"You sure?"

When she asked that, I kinda got angry. When I get drunk, I'm kinda aggressive.

"What do you mean 'am you sure'?" I said. I pointed to my boys, who had their heads dropped and appeared to be sleeping on the table. "Look at 'em. They gone. Don't you think we know our limits?" My pager started vibrating again. "And who the fuck keeps on paging me? Goddamn!!" The waitress walked off.

J woke up and started talking shit. "It's your woman," he said. "Better call her."

"You right," I said. "Be right back." I slipped off the stool and stumbled to the payphone. Keep in mind now that during the time this story is occurring it's 1991, and not everybody had a cell phone or a pager. So I stumbled to the phone, put the quarter in, and misdialed. Twice.

Dammit and shit! Even while I was dialing, the pager kept going off with her number in it. It was goin' off so much, that even I was goin' like, *What in the hell does she want, pagin' me this goddamn much?* Honestly, since I've known that girl, I ain't never -- and I mean NEVER --- known her to blow up my pager like that.

After nervously fumbling with the dial buttons on the phone for the third time, I got the number right and she picked up.

"Hello?" she said.

"What the fuck is your problem?" I ranted. "I told your ass I was coming. Why the hell you keep pagin' the hell outta my pager?"

"Where are you?" she asked. Clearly she couldn't care less about how I felt about her worryin' the shit outta me.

"Did you hear what I just said?" I said.

"Did you hear what the fuck I just asked?" she countered.

"I don't give a fuck what you just asked me! Why you keep blowing up my pager?" I screamed.

"Well, it's about an hour from the time that you said you were coming, and I was just wondering where you are." Just hearing this made me suspicious. Normally Kaci would've screamed back, but she was so levelheaded and cool that it made me think I was wrong for yelling at her.

"Why?" I asked. "You never wondered where I was before. Why now?" I played loosely with the phone cord. She didn't say anything. "HELLOOOO?" I shouted.

"Yeah, I'm still here. So when you think you might be coming?" she asked again.

"Don't know. Probably in an hour."

"An hour?!" she exclaimed, her voice rising with that annoyed Black woman voice.

"You heard me, goddammit. An hour it's gonna be. Is there a problem?"   There was a pause. Then, "No problem. Fine. I'll see you here in an hour."

I didn't say nothin', just hung up the phone. I walked back to our party and sat my black ass back down.

"You all right?" E.J. asked.

"Yeah. I'm cool."

"You sure?" Jeff asked.

"Yeah man. I said I was cool." I looked at the table. Empty pitcher, drained glasses, everybody's eyes half-lidded and heavy, not thinking on what would happen next. We were definitely faded, and I was sooo numb. Yep, we were about right.

"Ya'll 'bout ready?" I slurred.

"Yup," E.J. said, head back on the table.

"You know it," said Jeff, fumbling in his pockets for what I don't know.

Cool. We waited for the waitress to come back and bring the bill, paid for it, and then we were out.

Memorial Drive in Decatur is a good little ways from Norcross, so since I was driving, I decided to take my time. I was concerned about my life and putting my other car member's lives at risk. Nahhhh, let me top lying. I was really taking my time because I was so fucked up and couldn't really focus that well. But dammit, I had somewhere to be, and I was gonna get there. And if it meant driving only forty two miles an hour on the expressway, then dammit, that's what I had to do. Weaving into the other lanes and all.

So we rolled out and eventually made it over there, me driving all the way on autopilot. Don't know how long it had been, don't know how we got there in one piece, but the numbness was starting to wear off and I was starting to feel my face again. It was winter and the hawk was out. We had the radio blasting and the heat up all the way, so you know that these were ideal conditions in which to just crash and sleep. At least, that's what I felt like doing.

I parked the car, and looked over at the crew again. They had already taken my idea, 'cuz them fools were knocked out. Jeff was sitting in the front with his mouth wide open, and E.J. was laid across the back seat, snoring. I reached over to shake Jeff, and then turned around to shake E.J.

"Hey. Ya'll wake up. We're here." J. opened his eyes, and they were seriously bloodshot. But E.J. kept snoring. I shook his ass. "E! Wake up!"

"We're here?" Jeff asked.

"Yeah, we're here," I said. "Everybody up?"

"Straight," E.J. said, leaning up against the rear window.

"I'm fixin' to go up in there and see what this girl is talkin' about," I said. "Be back in a minute."

I opened the door and got out. Then that wind hit me and any numbness I might have had was all gone. It literally felt like someone had slapped me with an unlotioned hand. I tucked my coat tight and proceeded to make it up the steps to her apartment. When I got to the top, Jeff opened his door and was like, "Ay, when you get in there, ask her if you can use the phone so you can call the wife and tell her I'm with you."

"You got it," I said, turning back around. For a few seconds, I looked at the door, and a feeling of nervousness set into my stomach. I hesitated. Do I really want to know why she dissed me? Was this shit really worth my time? And why the fuck did she keep paging me?

Lo and behold, as soon as I thought about her paging me, the pager went off again. I surveyed it, and damn if it wasn't Kaci's ass again. That settled it. The nervousness subsided and I knocked on that damn door.

I heard someone coming down the steps and then opening up the door. It was no one else but her.

"Hi," she said. "Come on in." I stepped in and looked around.

"What?" she asked.

"What kind of bullshit trick are you up to?"

"No tricks," she said. "I just wanted to talk."

"Yeah? Just you and me, huh?"

"That's right." I looked around. It was dark. No noise anywhere.

"Where's your mom and bro?" I asked.

"Teddy's at a friend's house, and my mom's upstairs in her room."

"They doin' all right?"

"Yeah. Everyone's doin' fine."

"Good. Before we even get started, I wanted to know if I could use your phone to make this important call," I said. "Is that gonna be all right?"

"Yeah. You can use the phone in my room," she stated, walking in front of me and leading the way.

We walked up the stairs and when we got to the room, she opened the door. As it slowly parted, my mouth opened in amazement. I was looking at a bed with colored lights on stands surrounding it, like it was a stage production. You know, the kind of lights that you see on stage? That's what I saw, and it tripped me out.

"So where'd you get this from?" I asked.

"What you mean, *'where'd I get this from?'*" Kaci snapped. "I worked for it."

"Not at a fast-food restaurant," I said. "'I know for a fact that fast food don't pay you enough for this."

All of a sudden, I heard a click, and I knew that meant her mom was locking her door (they had adjoining rooms), probably because she didn't want to get involved with her daughter's affairs. Thought she wasn't at home? Here we go with the lying again.

"It does, and it's all mine," she said.

Now what?

Meanwhile, on the outside of the apartment (as told to me later by E.J. and Jeff), a car pulled right next to mine with two guys in it. Jeff and E.J. were awake by then, and just listening to the radio. Now while I was inside, according to J, the driver and passenger looked over at them, and then the driver got out. He was tall, light-skinned and lanky, and had a scar on his right cheek. His boy was dark-skinned, with a mouth like a pot o'gold, 'cuz (according to J), every time he opened his mouth to talk, you saw a shine coming through.

Both of 'em looked suspicious. The driver had on all black, with a long black overcoat. He closed the door and looked up at the apartments. Then he walked around to where Jeff was sitting. J rolled the window down.

"What's up?" Jeff asked.

"Ain't nothin'" he said. He looked in and saw E.J. sittin' in the back. I think he was tryin' to size up some thangs, just in case some shit went down. "Ummm…ya'll know Kaci Mc--- or know where she stay at?"

My cousin, who kinda felt that vibe that the dude was up to no good was like, "Who?"

"Kaci."

"I don't know who that is," J. said.

"Who's Kaci?" E.J. asked.

"Never mind."

And just like that, he walked straight up to her apartment. My cousin, being a cop, watched him.

"Now if he didn't know where that bitch stayed, how'd he know where to go to?" Jeff asked E.

"Don't know," said E.J. "Somethin's up. Know what I mean?"

"Unh huh. I got that feelin', too. Keep your eyes on that other boy." Meanwhile, on the inside, I had sat down to use the phone to call Jeff's wife when I heard the doorbell ring.

What the? I said to myself.

Kaci came running back up the stairs and busted open the door.

"You've gotta go. My boyfriend's here!" she said breathlessly.

"Boyfriend?" I asked in amazement. "You said you ain't had no boyfriend."

"Well I do, so you've gotta get outta here."

I stood up, heart beating fast as hell. "So what was the point of me coming over here? We ain't gonna talk?"

"Unh unh. You gotta get outta here. Now. He got a bad temper."

She started out the door and I followed her down the steps. The driver (who was also her boyfriend) was now inside, waiting at the door, trying to look menacing with his all black on and his hands stuck in his pocket.

When Kaci got to him, she hugged and kissed him. I had stopped one step in front of him, staring directly into his eyes. He put his hand around her waist and squeezed her butt.

"This him?" the dude asked, with Kaci smiling.

"Yeah," she said. Something *was* up. He looked me up and down. I was fired up.

"So what's up then?" I asked them both.

Kaci had stepped away from him and was watching both of us to see what we were gonna do. It was almost like watching an illegal dogfight (which I absolutely fuckin' hate), in which we were pitted against each other for a bloody outcome.

Dirty bitch.

"Nothin' mu'fucka." The driver still had his hands in his jacket pockets, still keeping his jacket closed. "'Sup with you?" he asked.

"So you her man?" I asked.

"Yeah."

"Yeah? She told me she didn't have nobody," I told him. "So you need to check your girl. She called me and told me she wanted to see me; not the other way around."

Dude laughed. "Hey asshole, you think she really wanted to see you? *I* told her to call you 'cuz I wanted to see the mu'fucka that was harassin' her."

"Harassin' her?" I looked at Kaci in disbelief. "What the fuck is he talkin' about? I ain't been harassin' you!"

"Yes you have," she said. "You been botherin' me for a long-ass time." Liar!

"That's right, bitch," he said to me. "And that's why I'mmo end all this unnecessary. Tonight."

"Oh yeah?" I asked, looking him up and down again.. "You and who else? You just a lil' mu'fucka, so you just might be catchin' an ass whuppin', fuckin' with me tonight," I said, staring directly into his eyes. "'Cuz lemme tell ya: somebody's goin' to the hospital, and guess what? Ain't gonna be me."

"It ain't gonna be me neither mu'fucka," he said. Ya'll, this was seriously a little dude. He looked like Al B. Sure minus a hunnerd pounds. Looked like a strong wind could blow him away on a windy day. But here he was, trying to act like he could do some damage.

"So whassup then?" I asked again. "What you wanna do, little dude?"

Then, without hesitation, he opened up his coat, and damn if it wasn't a gun lodged in there. And we ain't talkin' just any gun either. I could tell by the butt that it was definitely a shotgun. A sawed-off one, too. Shorter length for greater damage, and illegal as well.

That's why her mom locked her door: She didn't want to be a witness to this; what-was-supposed-to-be a pre-meditated murder.

Meanwhile on the outside, after seeing the driver going to the door and going in, Jeff told E.J., "Man…something's wrong. I'm goin' in."

"But what about this dude still sittin' here?" E.J. asked. "He might try to come behind you."

"If that's the case," J said, pulling a 38 from under his pants leg, "Use this." He handed E.J. the gun.

E looked at it, cocked it and pointed it out the window into the other car. The other dude wasn't even payin' attention. He had his sights still set on watchin' the apartment.

"You know how to shoot?"

"Shoot yeah. I was on the ROTC rifle team in college."

"So you know, then?"

"Yeah. I know."

"Good," Jeff said, getting out of the car. "Just cover me." He closed the door and E.J. moved over to the driver's side in the back and sat ready, just in case this dude decided to go help his boy. Sure enough, when the passenger saw Jeff getting out and walking up the stairs, he tried to unlock his door. And that's when E.J. rolled the window down and cocked back.

"Ay man, you better stay your ass in that car," he said. Passenger dude just looked at him, caught completely off-guard. "And lemme see your hands." The passenger dude held his hands up. "Now put them mu'fuckas on the door and keep 'em there. Otherwise I'ma put an extra hole in your ass." The passenger stayed seated, hands on the window.

Back on the inside, I was scared and angry at the same time. I had walked into a setup, just like in the movies. Kaci hadn't called me to talk; rather, she wanted me to come over because she wanted me eliminated; not just from her life, but off the face of the earth. But I wasn't backing down. I looked at Kaci, and my eyes were like daggers.

"Is this what it's come down to, Kaci?" I asked. "You tryin' to kill me? You think you're gonna get away with this, scott-fuckin' free?"

"I ain't gonna do it." She kissed her boy on the cheek. "*He's* gonna do it."

"Yeah? Well, he ain't gonna get away with it. Somebody always talks, and sooner or later, somebody's gonna come lookin' for me, so fuck both of ya'll. Now what?"

"Shit Al, ain't nobody gon' be lookin' for you," Kaci said, looking lovingly at her boy, who was also my potential killer. "We've taken care of thangs to make sure of that, Will and I."

Will, huh? Mistake number one: If I make it out alive, I can tell the cops exactly who he is and what he looks like. Emaciated Al B. was coming to do me in.

"Will huh?," I said. "Well Will, lemme tell you something. Everyone pays for what they do in the end. And what you may think about doin' to me, when dealing with this bitch, she might decide to have this same thing done to you once she gets tired of you. You need to think about that, brotha. As you can see, this is a dirrrrty bitch right here. And she ain't doin' nothin' but settin' you up for failure. Can't you see that?"

By now, Kaci was tired of me talkin' to him. "Just shut the fuck up, Al!" she screamed. "You sicken me. Will, take him with you so you can handle this business." Will kissed her again.

"You right baby. He almost convinced me." Will didn't even take his hands out of his pockets. Instead, all he asked me was, "So back to business. You ready to die, bitch?"

When he said that, the fear had left me, with anger quickly replacing it.

"Fuck it," I said. "Let's do it. If I was meant to die, it was gonna happen anyway. I ain't afraid of you, punk. So go ahead, pull the trigger!"

And then the doorbell rang.

Kaci opened up the door, and there stood Jeff, looking like a bad-ass Black cowboy, straight out of a western. He had his cowboy hat on, his suede jacket, and a big-ass cowboy belt buckle with HIS gun tucked behind it.

Got-damn, the cavalry was here and just in time! I breathed a sigh of relief.

"Can I help you?" Kaci asked him.

"Yeah," Jeff said. "You don't know me, but I'm Al's cousin. Now, I don't know what kind of shit's about to go down, but I'ma let you know two goddamn thangs. One, this (pointing to me) is my cousin, as well as my boy, so I ain't gonna let shit happen to him. Two, I am a cop, which means that I'm licensed to shoot, so why don't you tell your homeboy to get the fuck outta here before I fill you and him full of fuckin' holes?"

Will looked directly at Kaci, sighed, closed up his coat, and told her, "Sorry, girl. Maybe next time." Then he walked his ass out of the door.

"Will," she called to him.

Jeff looked at me. "Told you this bitch was crazy. Let's go," he said, walking back down the steps and shaking his head.

I didn't say another word. I followed Jeff down the steps who followed Will to make sure he got in his car, and saw E.J. with the gun still pulled on the passenger, who by now must have had hypothermia because his hands were on that door for so long with the windows rolled down.

"Hey E," J called out. "You can let that shit go. Him and Mr. Will was just leaving. Right, Mr. Will?"

Will didn't say anything because he knew that it had been a bullshit plan. He just got in the car, crunk it up and left. We stood there for a minute. I was shook.

Jeff looked at me. "You okay, man?"

No, I wasn't. With the realization that Kaci set me up to actually have me murdered kicking in, the feeling of wanting to do something to her like beating her ass rose up in me.

"'Ay, Al," J asked again. "Come on man. You ready to go?"

"Hell, naw," I said slowly, reality kicking in. "This bitch tried to set me up to get killed. Fuck that. I can't let that ride."

In that instant, I don't know what came over me, but I took off, bolting back up the stairs to her apartment, not knowing what I was getting ready to do. But I was determined I was gonna do *something*.

Between the time Jeff came to the door and forcing Will to leave, Kaci had just been watching what was going on. Now as I ran up the stairs to bust that ass, I moved so fast that she was in a state of shock and couldn't close the door quick enough. I mean, she was really shocked.

"Al!" Jeff and E.J. both called out. I could hear, but I wasn't paying them a bit of attention.

"Fuck this!" I said, as I finally reached the top where her door was. Kaci stood there terrified, like she didn't know what I was gonna do to her. The bitch tried to reason with me.

"Now Al, hold up. I didn't mean…" Kaci stammered.

But it was too late. I didn't have no gun (good thing too, 'cuz I think I probably would've shot her and her momma had I had one), but I looked down and there were rocks. I picked 'em up too, and just started throwing them and cussing her at the same time.   "You fuckin' bitch!" I yelled out. "Dirty fuckin' bitch tried to set me up to get killed, and didn't deny it either! You ain't shit, you fuckin' piece of black country trailer trash!" I yelled out, steadily pitchin' like John Smoltz.

I was almost out of rocks, but some empty bottles were around. Every time I threw something, Kaci closed the door to shield herself. But right after, she'd open up the door and yell out, "Fuck you, mu'fucka! Fuck you!"

All this drama and her sorry-ass excuse for a mother never left the comfort and safety of her own bedroom. Guess she didn't want to be a witness, and now that Kaci's bullshit plan had been foiled, she probably didn't wanna get fucked up either. 'Cuz I swear, if that goddamn girl and her momma would've come outside to try and confront me, somebody would've either gone to the hospital or to the morgue. And guess what? It damn sure wouldn't have been me.

So I'm still yelling and throwing at the door.

"And your bitch of a momma ain't shit either, you fuckin' cunt! You tried to kill me, so bring your ass out here and let's go! Wasn't countin' on nobody being here but me, huh bitch?!"

All this going on, and not one of her neighbors turned their lights on or came out to see what was going on. Guess they saw drama like this all of the time but figured it was best not to get involved. Good thing too, 'cuz they wouldn't have wanted none of this.

Finally, Kaci gon' yell out to me with the door halfway open, "Get the fuck off my property or I'll call the police! I mean it, stupid ass mu'fucka!"

"You stupid bitch, there's a policeman right down in the parking lot! And he's my cousin, you ignorant-ass bitch!" I shot back. "So what now?"

"I'll call the other police, and they'll get all of ya'll's asses outta here!" she yelled. "They'll make ya'll mu'fuckas move!"

By now, Jeff figured that he'd let me have a little time to vent and work out my frustration. As long as I didn't cause bodily harm or hurt nobody, it was cool. But since he saw the energy between us (i.e., that colorful exchange of words, my pitching arm with earthy materials), he headed up the stairs, unbeknownst to me.

I was in a rage, and the only thing I thought about was all the bullshit that just went down. I was getting ready to go from pitching and verbal abuse to actually getting physical. And when she threatened to get us out of there by callin' up the cops, well, that's when I just lost it. I even stopped throwing.

"Call the cops?" I asked. "Naw. You the one talkin' all that shit. Come out here and *make* us move, bitch! But I'm fixin' to kick your fuckin' door down, and I'm gonna kill your ass!"

And with that, Kaci closed the door and I was off and running full speed to tear that fucking door off the hinges and beat the shit outta that girl. Don't get me wrong, I don't hit women. But tryin' to get me killed? I'm sure that you as the reader might agree: In this case, Kaci had it coming.

That's when Jeff tackled me from behind and wrestled me to the ground. "Fool, you done lost your mind!" he yelled out. "We gotta get the fuck up outta here!"

"That bitch has an ass-whuppin' comin! Let me go, goddammit!" I struggled, but he had me good.

"Take that bitch somewhere else!" Kaci yelled out. I was still struggling to break free.

"You see that Jeff? That's why! Bitch, fuck you!" I screamed out to her. "That bitch gotta pay!" I said, still struggling to get loose.

"Dog, she's gonna pay," Jeff said. "Believe me, that shit will come back. Karma is a mu'fucka. Bad things happen to bad people. Just give it time."

"Man, fuck time!" I sputtered. "That bitch needs to pay now!"

Jeff still didn't let me go. "Al, if you don't calm your hostile ass down I will drag you down these steps, cuff you, and throw your ass in the backseat. So for the last time, calm your drunk ass down! I mean it!"

It seemed like an eternity 'cuz I was still resisting. My neck started to hurt and my back started to ache from laying on the pavement in the cold. But slowly, the anger in me started to subside. I started to relax and stop resisting.

Jeff felt me relax and eased his hold. "You calm now?"

"Yeah man. Let me up."

"You sure? 'Cuz if I have to run and chase you down again, I'm gonna treat you like a criminal and your car like a cruiser. So again: Are...you...calm?"

"Yes...I...am," I answered. "So...let...me...go. I won't run to this bitch again."

He finally released me and we walked down to the car. I got in the back, Jeff got in the passenger's seat, and E.J. was in the driver's seat.

"Drive," J told E.

He crunk up and we were outta there.

Nobody said anything for the rest of the night, and after that situation, I never called, thought about, or wondered about how Kaci was, ever again. From that point on, Kaci was dead to me. And that's how I wanted her to stay.

EPILOGUE

So what did I learn from this incident? Plain and simple, the girl was cra-zay! Kaci was nothing but a manipulator and opportunist, and a good one at that. When things got too crazy between us, I think she started looking for a way out. And she did that by lying to me and Will about everything. And he was probably so blinded by her looks and the booty that he believed *everything* she told him, including that I was harassing her. Just like me.

But here's what I learned: Just 'cuz a chick looks good don't necessarily mean that she's right in the head. Beauty fades, booty spreads and acquires dimples, breasts eventually feel that pull of gravity and go from being perky to eggs on a nail, and wrinkles and varicose veins start populating the body like interstates. But in the end, it's really what's in the dome that counts.

Personally, I would rather have a cutie who's intelligent and on the same page with me when it comes to the same goals and dreams as I have instead of that trophy chick who's crazy as hell and is all for self (um, like Kaci).

My dad once told me the prettier women are, the crazier they are, and that is so true. Things definitely get worse than better when dealing with this type of woman because somebody's gassed their heads up for so long about how good they look that they finally start to believe their own hype, and don't know anything else except how to be pretty. Yes…to all you women like this out there, all is definitely not well, is it? I'm sure that for some being a trophy chick is both a gift and a curse. You stay lonely, wishing for the one you want, but ignoring the ones that want you.

The last thing I learned from this relationship is that if your parents ain't 'bout nothin', then you probably ain't gonna be shit yourself. The only things that this girl had going for herself was that she had an exotic look with a big booty, and that she was a freak in the bed. She didn't graduate from high school (lied about that), worked at a fast-food restaurant and apparently couldn't see nothin' else past that for the future. Basically she used what she had to get what she wanted, living day to day and check to check. And I fell for that.

But I really blame that shit on her mom's best-friend-with-my daughter, hands-off rearing as well. Her mom wasn't hittin' on a damn thang. Just like Kaci, ol' girl didn't graduate from high-school, but went on to get a GED, went to nursing school and got certified. *Certified* ya'll, and lost her job on some bullshit that could've been prevented. As a result, her ass was now at the same place, working with her daughter. Damn if the fruit didn't fall too far from the tree in this case.

Finally, once a woman is fed up with things, that's pretty much about it. And once she chooses to get rid of you, it's a wrap. As you can see, she wanted to get rid of me, but in the most extreme way. If a woman wants to end things with you, get out while you can, or you might just suffer the same fate I almost did.

Believe me, it's an eerie feeling that still sends chills up my spine; even to this day, that what happened that night still creeps me out. Think about it: this woman was evil enough to try to set me up to get killed, and then tried to carry it out by getting her new man to be the hit man.

Man, when she did this, it let me know (and should send out a warning to the reader) to beware of people. You never truly know what people's intentions are, and you only see what they want to reveal. But God was with me that night, and to that I continue to be grateful. Otherwise, I would've been just another statistic.

But like my cousin said, karma does come back, and when it comes back it hits hard. Cut to the present: One day, my younger cousin Keid came over to the house, and out of the blue asked me did I date a girl named Kaci. When I said I did, he replied, "You know she's dead, don'tcha?" I was shocked, but didn't fully believe him. I asked what happened, and he said that she had had a brain aneurysm. Killed her instantly. And when I Googled it, there was an eternal candle funeral page on which her pictures were posted and replies from people that knew her. I told myself, *Well, I'll be damned.* It's true that there are indeed six degrees of separation or six people that we could talk to in order to find a person. And when my same cousin connected me to another person that knew her, I found out everything. Found that she dated Will for a little while after me, but then left him to be with the dj from Magic City, who was a part of the group Tag Team. The same group that did "Whoomp! There It Is!" After that dj dropped her, she dated many other dudes, but had finally settled on one, and tried to get her life right. But I guess that everything she did finally caught up with her, enough things for the Lord to call her home and have her to answer to him for everything she put dudes and her family through. Her life ended in 2015. And to that I say, how's *that* for karma? Everyone is accountable for what they do.

EVERYONE.

Including Kaci.

May she rest in peace.

www.ingramcontent.com/pod-product-compliance
Lightning Source LLC
Chambersburg PA
CBHW020606250626
47154CB00004B/1379